D1557515

By SAM CARLSON

A Glass of Red

Published by DREAMSPINNER PRESS
www.dreamspinnerpress.com

sam carlson

A Glass of Red

Published by

DREAMSPINNER PRESS

5032 Capital Circle SW, Suite 2, PMB# 279, Tallahassee, FL 32305-7886 USA
www.dreamspinnerpress.com

A Glass of Red
© 2021 Sam Carlson

Cover Art
© 2021 Stef Kloibhofer
www.stefkloibhofer.com
Cover content is for illustrative purposes only and any person depicted on the cover is a model.

Trade Paperback ISBN: 978-1-64405-910-4
Digital ISBN: 978-1-64405-909-8
Trade Paperback published April 2021
First Edition
v. 1.0

Printed in the United States of America
∞
This paper meets the requirements of
ANSI/NISO Z39.48-1992 (Permanence of Paper).

For Chris, who believed.

CHAPTER 1

NOAH FIDGETED as he stepped up onto the first, then the second, then the third step of the entrance to the villa. The steps, he noticed, were comfortably shallow and easy to climb: wide spans of what looked like pleasantly yellow sandstone reaching up to the front door. Pleasing to the eye mostly because of how well they accompanied the general orange-to-yellow tones of the villa itself, despite the dark brown shutters and the vivid red door.

Finally, he noticed that the main reason he'd taken in so many details about the stone steps was because he was staring at his feet.

Breathe, he told himself, *just breathe. How bad could it possibly be?*

The interview for the job had been harrowing, at least at first. He'd gone to meet Chester Cunningham at Mr. Cunningham's work as requested, but having only moved to New York a short time prior, he didn't really know his way around the city yet and failed to recognize the address. Standing in front of a skyscraper and taking the elevator up to a prestigious law firm that bore two separate Cunninghams in the name told him how far out of his element he was. The shy art student gulped as a secretary showed him into a big conference room with a beautiful window view.

What put him back at ease wasn't Mr. Chester Cunningham but rather his wife, Eloise. Where Mr. Cunningham had been insistent and even a little brusque, she was charming and kind. Mr. Cunningham had reined in his icy demeanor by "discussing" a schedule he expected Noah to follow while at the villa instead of "mandating" one. Eloise had done the opposite, reining in her politeness to try to be professional. Despite her efforts, though, Noah sensed that mothering was in her nature as she offered him chocolate chip cookie after cookie.

"Eloise, don't let the boy fill up on cookies," Chester Cunningham said, giving her a knowing wink. She smiled at Noah one more time as she set the plate down, leaving him wondering what a comment like that foreshadowed.

"We dearly love the house," Mr. Cunningham said, "but it needs work. There's a lot of hard work to be done, a lot of hard work."

"I'm not afraid of a little hard work, sir," Noah said. "I mean… I don't know what you had in mind, but…."

"Oh, none of that, dear," Eloise said reassuringly. "We've hired a handyman to fix up the place, Signor Caravelli, an older gentleman in the village nearby. He's been in and around the house through its last two owners, and he was really just a fantastic find. He says he'll have it ready for us by the fall and we can go for the holidays!"

"That sounds lovely, Mrs. Cunningham."

"Please, call me Ellie," she said through that beatific smile.

"*Mrs. Cunningham* and I," Mr. Cunningham said, emphasis clearly on his preferred way for Noah to address his wife, "do plan to spend the latter part of the summer there, possibly the holidays as well. The work we're interested in you for has to do with that, but not exactly with the house itself."

"Oh?"

"You're studying art history at NYU, yes?" Mr. Cunningham asked in a voice that said the old lawyer already knew the answer. "Graduate student? Waiting tables on the side, I'm led to understand?"

"Yes, sir. If the house has artwork you need inspected or appraised, I can help, but I'm sure—"

Cunningham waved that notion away. "Professionals have already been through what the previous owners left behind. But I'm told that you're also studying wine."

Noah nodded. Waiting tables was just a way to make the ends meet between classes, a lot of grad students did it, but he'd been taking evening classes with a sommelier because waiters who knew wine inside and out were hired at better restaurants, and for better pay.

"Oh, yes, sir. It's been a hobby of mine for a long time, and I've been taking classes. I've learned a lot. I don't want to wait tables all my life, but I figure if it'll pay better, then why not turn a hobby into something more?"

"Well I'm glad to hear that," Eloise said with a cheery look and a triumphant clap of the hand on the tabletop. "I like someone with ambition, no slouching your way through life."

Mr. Cunningham vigorously nodded agreement. "I feel the same."

There was a knock at the door, and Mr. Cunningham shouted, "Enter!" Noah, still a little on edge, though the talk of wine had relaxed him, jumped in his seat. Neither of the Cunninghams seemed to notice, or if they did, they were too polite to say anything.

The secretary that Noah had seen before entered the conference room, still smiling and wheeling a tray. On the tray were three covered dishes, silver cloches hiding their contents.

"Lunch!" Mr. Cunningham said, clapping his hands and rubbing them together. "Noah, I trust you'll join us?"

The not-quite-but-almost starving art student's mouth had already begun to water, so he nodded. Even if he didn't get whatever job it was they wanted him for, at least he might get a free lunch out of the meeting.

"That's very kind of you, sir. Thank you."

When the trays were served and uncovered, three chicken dishes were revealed. Eloise leaned over her dish and took a deep breath in, smiling over the plate of roasted bird with vegetables, and Mr. Cunningham did practically the same. It occurred to Noah that as a lunch meal it was a bit elaborate, but who knew? Maybe this was how rich people ate.

"Excellent!" Mr. Cunningham declared. His secretary handed him a sheet of stiff paper before leaving, which he read and then passed over to Noah.

"Noah, would you care to recommend a wine to have with lunch?"

Oh, now I get it, Noah realized as he took the sheet. It was a wine list. *This is a test.*

"Sure," he said and considered the sheet. Six vintages were listed, three whites and three reds.

There's a nice-looking Pinot Noir here, but that's a trap. You can serve Noir with roast chicken, but you'd want to do it with a heavy gravy or a sauce, and this little guy looks like he was roasted in his own juices.

For the same reason he immediately rejected the Côtes-du Rhône, as well as the Shiraz. All would be too heavy for the bird as it was presented.

There go all the reds, then, he thought with a sigh, preferring red himself when given the option. *White it is.*

He ignored the Zinfandel completely. While it was a fine enough wine, one he enjoyed himself when he had whites, its reputation of "going well with everything" wasn't one he felt would impress obvious connoisseurs like the Cunninghams. There was a Viognier on the list, and he almost picked it, knowing its aromatic qualities would introduce a whole new dimension to the lunch, but at the last second he changed his mind.

"Well, sir, there's a good-looking white Burgundy on the list, a 2003 Meursault les Chevalières. It's a mature wine with some savory complexity to it. I see there are mushrooms and truffles in the lunch, so it'll probably bring those out."

A look passed between the two Cunninghams that Noah couldn't quite read, and he got nervous.

"Perhaps," Mr. Cunningham finally said. "There's a nice Viognier there too, from Paso Robles. Why not that one instead?"

"I considered it," Noah said, nodding, "And it would be an excellent choice too. But the truth is that Viogniers are so aromatic and floral, I didn't want to overpower the chicken."

"You don't think it would've added a new dimension here?" Eloise asked.

We must watch the same shows on the Food Network, Noah thought.

"It would have, of course, Mrs. Cunningham. But that wasn't my goal. I picked a wine that I think will enhance the dish and the eating experience. Not one that would substantially change it."

Eloise's face changed into a smile of triumph, and the look she gave her husband was pure "I told you so." Mr. Cunningham's smile was more restrained, but he nodded and ordered the bottle of white Burgundy that Noah had recommended. When it arrived Mr. Cunningham poured, a glass for himself and one for Noah. Eloise took only half a glass. As they all tucked into their lunch, they sampled the wine and resumed the professional discussion.

"No doubt about it, Noah, you know your stuff," Mr. Cunningham said as he cut. Eloise nodded and agreed around a mouthful of chicken.

"Thank you, sir. I've only been studying for a while, but it's always been a hobby."

"Would you pursue it professionally?"

Noah paused and looked up from his meal. "Well, I mean, there is… there's my work in art that I love, it's a passion, not just a hobby—"

Mr. Cunningham waved him off. "I didn't mean like that. This is about the villa we were talking about, the one in Tuscany that needs work."

"Oh?"

"The previous owners had to vacate in a bit of a hurry," Cunningham said abruptly, as if he didn't wish to discuss their reasons, "which is why there's so much to be done. One thing they left behind, for us to take on at an impressively low price, was what we're told is a rather marvelous wine cellar. We're looking for someone to catalogue it, inspect for spoilage or other damage, and give us some sort of a reference document that we can give to our insurance company."

"And also for our own use," Eloise chimed in, "when we're at the villa trying to choose a bottle."

"Yes, of course," Mr. Cunningham agreed.

"Well, sir," Noah began, coughing to clear his throat, "I'm… I'm flattered, but surely you can afford someone a little more experienced?"

"What more experience do we need?" Cunningham countered. He finished a big bite of chicken and pushed his plate away. "It's a big job, I admit, lots of bottles down there, but not a difficult one. It'll be good experience that you can use in your field, and we'll pay you, of course. Two months room and board at the villa, with a cash amount at the end."

Eloise nodded.

Noah had thought about it… for maybe a full nanosecond. Waiting tables sure did suck, and while his parents did help out with tuition a little, it was never enough. He'd applied for a couple of grants but had no hopes that any of them would pan out. Now here he was with an offer of two months during the summer when classes were out, in Tuscany, room and board at a gorgeous villa included? And all he had to do to get a paycheck on top of that was write about wine?

Finishing his own chicken, he beamed back at both of them. "Where do I sign?"

"That's the spirit!" Mr. Cunningham said. Eloise tried once again to press a chocolate chip cookie on him, insisting he deserved dessert.

Now, three weeks later, his apartment sublet and his feet on the doorstep of the Cunninghams' new real estate, he was a little nervous. After all, the only person he was likely to see in the near future was old man Caravelli. He'd have to walk down to the village for any other human companionship.

The whole plane ride over, though, he'd been reminding himself that it was an adventure. Something to tell his grandkids, spending two months in Italy... if he ever got around to finding a husband and some kids to start with.

Clearing his throat and pushing his glasses firmly up onto his nose, Noah knocked on the door.

"GRANDDAD, I appreciate what you're trying to do here, but I'm just not interested. Thanks."

Christian got up off the couch and headed for his bedroom, hoping that would be an end to the conversation, but no such luck. His grandfather followed him.

"I won't have you lying about the house like this!" he shouted. Christian shut his bedroom door behind him, but Granddad was no respecter of doors. He burst through and continued to admonish him. "This is the prime of your life!"

He pursed his lips at the old man. "Granddad, what am I, thirteen? Don't just barge into my room!"

"Christian!" The old man threw up his hands and sighed. He sat down on the bed. In an effort at being conciliatory, so did Christian.

"When your father told me that he and your mother were discussing divorce, my heart broke," old Silvio said. He took Christian's hand. "I could not believe it. They were always so much in love."

Christian nodded. "I still don't believe it, Granddad. They'll figure it out."

"Which is why, when he asked if I would take you in, I said yes in a moment."

Christian knew that was not, strictly speaking, the whole truth. Granddad had been a little put out. But he also knew that to interrupt the old man would get him a paternal smack in the back of the head, so he kept his mouth shut.

"They love you so much. You know this," Silvio said in his heavily accented English. "They want only for you to be happy. To see you out of school but unsettled, bouncing from this to that and this to that...." He gestured with one hand, waving it back and forth. "It bothers them."

"Granddad, I liked my life!" Christian said. "I like Miami, all my friends are there, I was—"

"Bah!" the old man dismissed him. "You were a bum, a 'beach bum' like your father says. Even with your fancy degree!"

Christian opened his mouth but found he couldn't argue. His grandfather resumed his softer tone.

"Your mother and father, they love you," he said again. "They want only for you to find a nice job, maybe a nice girl or a nice boy, and to be happy."

"But they didn't want me living on their couch while they were trying not to get a divorce, is that it?"

His grandfather made a face. In the oldest and purest tradition of Italian Catholicism, "divorce" was still not a word he liked to hear.

"They send you to me while they figure things out," he finally said. "And they will! But while you are in Tuscany, you will make your living. You will make your way."

"Can't I just make gnocchi?" Christian asked, a mischievous little smile beginning at the corner of his mouth. Silvio smiled and laughed.

"Rascal! Here is what you can make: you can make an old man proud and uphold the family name. What do you think of that?"

Christian sighed. It looked like he wasn't going to be getting out of the summer job after all. He felt like a high school kid being thrown out of the house to go "build character." In his twenties with a bachelor's degree under his belt, it felt degrading. Not to mention that a job from his grandfather would necessarily include manual labor.

Old Silvio slapped one hand on his leg where the cast was still fresh. "I cannot work, cannot fulfill an obligation. You know this. That mean old horse knew just where to wound me so that he would injure both my leg and my pride. I cannot restore the old Mattioli villa on one leg. At my age, I am lucky I survived the fall."

"Granddad, you'll survive anything."

The old man laughed again, but the sound was far from light-hearted. "We'll see, eh? One day, not so much. One day."

A silent moment passed between them.

"A man must fulfill his obligations," his grandfather finally said, "or he is no man at all. Until I am healed, someone must do for me, *si*? Someone must uphold the Caravelli name. The family honor. You understand."

Christian sighed yet again. "Yeah, I get it, Granddad. I understand."

CHAPTER 2

NOAH FELT that knocking on the door was a little redundant, given how it pushed open a half inch at his touch. It was an old wooden door, painted bright red, with a dozen or so square panes of glass set into it, a white curtain billowing loosely on the other side for some small measure of privacy.

Which feels a little pointless if they don't lock their doors around here, he thought.

"Hello?" he called into the house. "My name's Noah, I'm... I'm the wine guy? I'm... allowed to be here?"

Through the translucent curtain, he saw a figure approach, and he instinctively took a step back. Noah believed in first impressions, and who knew what to expect from an elderly Italian handyman?

"Hi," the figure said in a masculine voice as he opened the door. "They told me to expect you."

Noah gulped.

The man before him was *not* an elderly Italian handyman. He looked to be about Noah's age, only graced with a very different physique. His skin was a deep, beautiful bronze, whether from natural complexion or tanned by the sun, Noah could not tell. Straight brown hair fell down just to the tops of his ears but was cut close underneath, almost shaved in the style that was so fashionable in America. All he wore was a pair of cutoff jean shorts and some leather flip-flop sandals, the broad expanse of his chest showing a dusting of dark hair and two round, browned nipples. He'd obviously been painting, given the streaks of paint on his hands, his abdomen, his thigh, one of his pecs....

The young man was smiling in a friendly, welcoming way, and it occurred to Noah not to get lost in the moment.

"Yeah, hi!" he said, his voice squeaking involuntarily, for which he cursed himself. "I mean, hi. I'm Noah."

The tan young man nodded. "The wine guy."

Noah chuckled. "You've heard of me!"

The attempt at humor having received no laughs, he pressed on. "And you are…?"

"Oh, yeah, sorry," the Adonis said sheepishly. "I'm Christian. Caravelli."

"Oh!" Noah was confused. "The Cunninghams told me to expect someone… older?"

"Nope, that's my granddad," Christian replied. "They hired him, but he was injured horseback riding, so I'm taking over for him."

"Sure," Noah said, nodding. That made sense. "Well, nice to meet you, then!"

He stuck out his hand to shake, which Christian took. The weather was already warm, Italian summer and all, but with his hand wrapped in Christian's warm palm, it was all Noah could do not to break out in a sweat.

"Jeez, I'm sorry," Christian said, pulling his hand back. "I got paint on your hand."

Noah looked down. Sure enough, his hand was smeared with white paint.

He shrugged. "It comes off, right?"

"It does," Christian replied. He pointed behind Noah. "Is that your bag?"

Noah had traveled as light as possible, one rolling suitcase, even if it was rather large, into which he'd crammed clothes, laptop, wine guide, the essentials.

"Yeah, but—" He moved in between Christian and the bag as the handyman reached for it. "But maybe I'd better get it. Wet paint and all."

Christian laughed, and the sound was so full and beautiful, it was like a low, sonorous bell ringing somewhere deep within Noah's soul. They locked gazes, and Noah was lost in the deep chestnut brown of Christian's bedroom eyes.

"Maybe you'd better," he said, and he swung the door wide to admit Noah entry to the villa.

CHRISTIAN HAD expected his grandfather, and he'd been ready for a blowup. Having inspected the house, he was spoiling for the chance to tell his granddad exactly what he thought of the old man giving him so much work to do, when he'd opened the door to a sight that practically took his breath away.

The young man he'd allowed into the Cunningham villa, now following him through the entryway into the house proper and towing his suitcase as he did so, was just compelling somehow. It wasn't his sandy blond hair, Christian reflected, because he saw enough of that in Miami. By the same token, it wasn't the blue eyes, piercing though they were behind the black-framed glasses. And his slight, swimmer's build that Christian detected under the short-sleeved plaid button-down and cargo shorts, a body type in sharp contrast to the muscle-bound studs that usually filled Christian's evenings, was yet another feature that was attractive but hardly, in his opinion, mind-blowing.

It's that smile, he realized. That sheepish, slightly awkward smile that gave away a lifetime of being "the nerd" or "the sensitive one." A man who didn't even know how good-looking he really was. It was something Christian found a little adorable and couldn't quite get over.

As they rounded the corner toward the guest bedrooms, he noticed that he was smiling himself at the thought of it and couldn't remember when that smile had crept onto his lips. He thanked his lucky stars that his back was to the new arrival and it wouldn't be visible to... to....

Noah.

The name came back to him in an instant, and he allowed his smile one last gasp before stifling it.

We're both professionals, he chided himself. *Here to do a job. The last thing this poor guy wants, after hours on a plane and then hours more getting to the house by bus or whatever, is someone creeping on him.*

"My room's at the end of the hall," he said, pointing to the third guest room out of four. Not coincidentally it was also the biggest one. Christian had told himself when he chose it that it was a fair reward for being the first of the hired help to show up. He pushed open a door on the right side of the hallway, closest to the central part of the house. "This one's yours, unless you don't like it."

"I'm sure it's..." Noah began, though his voice cut off when he actually looked inside. Christian winced.

The room was in a sorry state of disrepair. The walls and the roof looked stable, but that was about all anyone could say for it. The paint was peeling almost everywhere, the closet door was hanging by one hinge, and the bare stone floor had been swept but was still dusty and grimy. There was a bed with sheets that looked clean, and a working desk that looked shabby but not a total disaster. A pair of french doors looked out onto a concrete walkway surrounding a pool... or they would have, if the panes of glass hadn't been dirty, cracked, or just plain missing.

"...fine," Noah finished, though from his tone Christian didn't believe him. "I'm sure it'll be just fine."

"There are two others," Christian said. "You can take a look at them if you want to. They're actually worse, though. I really think you're going to want this one."

Noah stood up a little straighter, steeling himself. Comparing their heights, Christian guessed that Noah was about five eight or five nine, as compared to his six one. Then he shook himself to drive those thoughts away once more.

"Thanks, I appreciate the thought," Noah said. His tone had regained some confidence, or at least a desire to make the best of things. "Where's the bathroom?"

Christian gulped. "Well, that's the thing. Each bedroom has its own bathroom, even the guest rooms, but—"

"Thank goodness," Noah said, wheeling his suitcase into the room and dropping both it and his leather satchel onto the bed. He walked right to the door of the bathroom and stopped. Christian watched from the doorway, stifling a laugh.

"Okay," came the voice from the bathroom door. Christian peeked around the corner to see Noah looking down. "Where's the toilet?"

"I, uh, I was getting to that," Christian replied.

Noah turned, his face ashen, clearly having viewed the serviceable bathtub and shower but also the hole in the ground where a toilet would go.

"The plumbing is ancient," Christian explained, "and most of the fixtures were not salvageable. There are two working toilets in the house right now, the one off the master bedroom—" He pointed back the way they'd come. "—on the far end of the house, or the nearer one—" He pointed down the hall. "—in… in my room. You're welcome to use the one in my room any time you want. I'm really sorry about this."

Noah turned back to the bathroom, as if trying to once again summon the strength to make the best of it.

"I guess I could just pee in the hole," he finally said. "If the plumbing will stand it."

Christian laughed. "Yeah, if you want to, you could do that."

Then Noah laughed, and Christian finally felt like they were off on the right foot.

CHAPTER 3

NOAH SPENT the rest of the day settling into his new accommodations. Despite its lack of a working door, the closet had both drawers and a place to hang things. He gave the drawers a quick swipe with one of the many dusting cloths lying around the place and then unpacked.

To his amazement, the bed wasn't that bad. Christian had told him that the Cunninghams had ordered some of the furniture before realizing what a state the place was in, which meant the two of them could benefit. His two-month adventure would at least allow him a comfortable night's sleep.

He set up his laptop at the desk and was surprised to find working wireless internet. Another thing that had been paid for ahead of time, it turned out. A chat with Christian soon yielded the password, and Noah was able to email his parents back in Ohio that he'd arrived safely.

Even though he had done everything to put Noah at ease and welcome him, Noah's thoughts about Christian were starting to make him uncomfortable. The guy was hot… as in *hot*. Noah just couldn't ignore it. That smile, those abs… the way his skin looked kissed by the sun… the way Noah felt when he put "Christian" and "kiss" in the same sentence….

"No," he said aloud to his empty room, as if to convince himself more than anyone in particular. He was here to work. The hot handyman eye candy, wandering around the house in his cutoffs to paint things and supervise plumbers and workmen, that was just one more perk of this fabulous job.

Noah spent the afternoon exploring the villa. He saw the grand entryway, decorated in a tasteful rustic style that was subdued rather than ostentatious, with what looked like vintage tile on the floor and all of it miraculously intact. He went through the door to the kitchen, but before inspecting that, he stopped to look at a small mosaic, about 11"x14", near the entry from the kitchen to the pool. It depicted a stylized merman in profile. To his critical art-history eye, it was obviously a modern, contemporary installation, but it fit the decor well enough. He stepped through the doors to the pool patio and found its inspiration: on the bottom of the murky-looking water, he could just make out Poseidon, god of the sea, depicted with a fishy tail of his own running the length of the pool.

"Hey there, old boy," he said, smiling at the god of the ocean depths laid out in tile below. "Nice to know someone's keeping an eye on things."

Apart from the general state of disrepair and the murky water, the layout of the pool was actually quite pretty. In a style not unusual to traditional Tuscan architecture, it was set into the ground inside a courtyard, bounded on all four sides by walls but open to the sky above. There were three entrances: the pair of dingy french doors he'd found from his own room, a better-looking pair that led from the pool to the backyard patio, and a single door from the kitchen composed of more panes of glass. Opposite the kitchen, the wall with no openings instead had an elaborate marble fountain depicting, once again, Poseidon.

Noah looked out and up, through the courtyard opening to the sky, which was a beautiful shade of blue. He imagined it wouldn't be fun to swim there in the rain, but on a nice sunny day like the one they were having, it could be pure heaven.

He returned to the kitchen and breathed a sigh of relief when he saw that it was clean enough to use. There were a few modern appliances, like a new refrigerator, but it still had a very rustic feel. A window over the sink looked out on the pool, and another pair of french doors went from the end of the kitchen out onto what looked like a dining patio. It occurred to Noah that Christian, who'd been living here who knew how long, had probably been the one to tidy the kitchen.

Another little smile crossed his face when he thought of Christian, that welcoming look on his lightly paint-splattered face as he'd opened the front door, but Noah pushed it away.

He found the door to the wine cellar and almost went down immediately to start work, but he stopped himself. There'd be time enough for that later. He wasn't procrastinating, he told himself, just getting to know the place before putting his nose to the grindstone.

The master bedroom was, as Christian had predicted, a bit of a hike to get to. The villa had only one level, but it was big, and the master bedroom was on the far opposite end. Noah walked past the dining room, the library, a study, and what he assumed was a living or music room in order to get to it. Once there, though, it didn't disappoint. Easily the same size as his New York apartment, it had high ceilings with exposed beams that looked like they were in excellent condition, compared to the rest of the home. One door led to a dual-sink bathroom with a beautiful sunken marble bathtub, and two other sets of doors led outside. Through one he saw a flowered garden, and the other looked like it went to the same entertaining patio that could be accessed from the kitchen.

There was no furniture, only drop cloths, and it was apparent that this was the room Christian had been painting when Noah had interrupted him. The wall farthest from him was an unsightly shade of brown while the other three were crisp white, and the wall nearest him was shiny, as if it might still be tacky to the touch. It begged the question where Christian was. If Noah had interrupted his work....

"Behind!" came a voice from behind him, and Noah quickly stumbled out of the way.

Christian walked down the hallway toward the bedroom, a cheery smile on his face that said he was just being polite, carrying several implements. He had two cans of paint in one hand and a stepladder tucked under his other arm. More noticeably, he had changed his outfit. Instead of all that skin on display, he now wore a pair of painter's coveralls, white but worn from years of use. Noah noticed they barely fit him, riding up well above his ankles and wrists, and he couldn't help but laugh.

"I'm sorry," he said. "That was rude."

Christian wrinkled his brow. "What?"

"It's... what are you wearing?"

"Oh," Christian said, chuckling in reply. "Yeah, these are Granddad's painting coveralls. He's kind of a little guy, I guess."

"Apparently."

"I figured, well, you know," Christian went on as he set down the cans of paint. "Now that I'm not the only one in the house anymore, maybe I shouldn't run around like it's my own personal playground."

"I don't mind," Noah said, and cursed himself for saying it so quickly. "I mean, hey, you do you. As big as this place is, we probably won't see much of each other anyway, right? I'll be in the basement, going through the wine cellar for hours on end, and you'll be up here."

"Oh, I'll be all over," Christian assured him. "But if you really don't mind, then thanks. I appreciate it. Italian summers, y'know."

He trailed off as if Noah were supposed to know what summers felt like in Italy from a wealth of personal experience, which Noah absolutely did not, but he nodded anyway. "For sure!"

Christian set up the stepladder in a far corner and started to unbutton the jumpsuit. It wasn't long before all that tan skin was visible once again, with the cutoffs that seemed to be less about clothing and more about just protecting his modesty.

Noah bit his lip and shook himself. *No!* he reminded himself. *Don't stare!*

THANK GOODNESS, Christian thought as he literally peeled out of the coveralls. Not only was it way too hot to be wearing the bulky things, as evinced by the way they'd already begun to stick to his skin, but he'd downplayed to the wine guy just how badly they didn't fit. For one thing, the way they rode up put serious pressure on his crotch that Christian just wasn't willing to handle for the long term.

He'd been afraid that Noah would be a little on the prudish side, just a vibe he had gotten. Maybe Christian was stereotyping based on his pseudo-nerdish image, but something about the wine expert definitely seemed... restrained. That was a good word.

None of my business, he reminded himself, and returned to the task at hand. The villa was structurally sound, and the master bedroom walls were no exception, but they were badly in need of new paint. He'd already stripped them as bare as he could without doing damage and was putting on the primer. Once that was done he could afford to move on to a serious paint job.

He was surveying the farthest wall from the door, the only one yet to be touched, when he realized the hairs were still up on the back of his neck. He looked over his shoulder and saw Noah there, still leaning in the doorway where he'd been when Christian arrived.

"Was there something else you needed?" he asked.

"Oh no," Noah stammered. "Sorry. The place looks great. The white really brightens it up."

Christian nodded. "I think so too. This is just a base primer. The Cunninghams picked out something a little more sandy and yellowish, but I think I'm going to send them a photo of what it looks like now. See if maybe they'd prefer white."

"Sounds good," Noah said. He stood up. "Guess I'd better go do what they're paying me for, take a look at that wine cellar. It's not, like, dangerous or anything, is it? Mold or mildew?"

"The inspectors cleared it," Christian said hesitantly, "but I'll be honest with you. I don't like it much down there. Smells... damp. And there might be mice."

Noah got that same ashen look he'd had when he realized there was no toilet in his bathroom, and again Christian suppressed a smile.

"What about... rats?" he asked.

"Oh, no way," Christian assured him. "A couple little mice here or there maybe, but no one's ever seen a rat here." He raised three fingers. "Scout's honor."

Noah wrinkled his brow and smiled. "You were in the Scouts? I have to say, your English is perfect."

Christian laughed. "It should be. Granddad lives here, just over in the village, but I'm not from here. My parents live in Florida and that's where I was born. I grew up in Miami."

"Oh!" Noah said. "Heh. That explains it, then."

"Yup."

They stood for an awkward moment, and Christian couldn't help but appraise Noah as they did. He wondered what Noah looked like underneath that plaid shirt, or maybe underneath elsewhere. If he was giving Noah the once-over, he thought, was Noah doing the same to him? Him, with a lot more on display?

"Anyway, yes, right!" Noah said, breaking the silence at last. He gave a nervous laugh that Christian didn't quite know how to interpret. "Thanks for the heads-up about the mice, and I'll head off down to the wine cellar!"

He went back along the hall the way he came, and Christian shook his head. For a second there, he'd thought maybe he'd detected something… the wine nerd coming on to him a little bit? Or at least attracted?

He shrugged and turned back to his painting.

CHAPTER 4

THE WINE cellar was exactly where Noah expected, through the door off the kitchen just where you'd want it, but he was unprepared for the full extent of the spacious, cavernous room. The stone walls had been carved out of an actual cave decades ago for exactly this purpose, presumably by the architect who designed the villa for its first owner, but it seemed to run the entire length of the house. As Noah looked off into the distance, he saw rack after rack, row after row of bottles of wine.

"I'm going to be here forever," he said in a low voice. He almost thought he could hear it echo.

The rack nearest to him was filled with bottles he instantly recognized: well-known labels that ran the gamut from high-priced staples of any collection to more moderately priced vintages that even the rich and famous might serve as table wines. He assumed these had been added the most recently by the Cunninghams.

As he started to walk the rows, the true enormity of the job continued to assault him. *These wines don't need a cataloger, they need a caretaker*, he thought. Some of them were old enough to need regular turning. It would be up to him to establish a schedule that the Cunninghams' regular staff could keep to.

That is, if they don't hire a full-time person just for the wine, he thought.

The cellar was damp, as Christian had warned him, and he did see a few mousetraps. But it was blessedly cool, pleasantly so, and Noah realized that he hadn't noticed how hot it really was upstairs. It occurred to him that was what Christian probably meant with his earlier comment.

Part of him wanted to head back to his room, grab his laptop, and start making notes right away. The sensible, logical side of him said that the only way to achieve a task this size was to begin immediately and make regular, steady progress. The romantic side of him, however, insisted that there was nothing wrong with enjoying a moment. That was the side that won, and he spent the next hour walking up and down the rows, stopping to inspect this or that bottle when one struck his fancy, and reveling in the idea of spending two whole months engaged in one of his favorite hobbies.

With Christian running around too.

When he finally did come up for air, the sun had begun to set. Noah, who was still wide-awake thanks to the time difference while traveling, found himself hungry. He wondered whether Christian would mind him grabbing something from the refrigerator and resolved to find out.

"Hello?" he called out as he walked down the hall to the master bedroom. "Christian, are you still in there?"

"Hi!" called the cheerful voice in reply, and as Noah came out into the room proper, he saw the half-dressed handyman, splattered with even more paint than before.

"Hey!" Noah said. "I didn't mean to interrupt. How's the wall going?"

"Great!" Christian replied. He stepped back and gestured wide with one arm to show off his handiwork, smiling like a proud third grader. The wall was almost finished, a few remaining spots only needing final touches.

"Nice job," Noah said. "I wanted to ask, the Cunninghams said room *and* board…. Is there food that's for sharing or, y'know, what was the plan?"

"For sure," he said. "Anything in the refrigerator is fair game, always. Feel free. They sent my granddad a stipend for food and there's a sweet lady in town named Maria who sends food up every Tuesday. As far as the wine goes they said that anything from the new rack was fair game. I figured you'd know which one they meant."

"I know exactly the one," Noah said.

"Fantastic." Christian grimaced. "There is one thing, though…. I don't know about you, but… let's just say I inherited a lot of things from my Italian grandfather and he taught me a bunch of skills, but cooking isn't one of them." He threw up his hands apologetically.

"That's no problem at all!" Noah said. "I can cook."

"You can? Like, no offense but…."

"I'm a great cook, Christian. I was just thinking about dinner. Are you hungry?"

Christian considered. "Sure, sounds good. We can get to know each other over a nice meal!" He looked at the wall. "Let me finish up here, take a shower, meet you in the kitchen?"

"It's a plan. What do you like?"

"Anything," Christian said, waving a hand dismissively. "Mom says I eat like a trash compactor."

"Heh." Noah laughed. "Okay, then. I'll go get started." He walked back toward the kitchen to see what he had to work with.

CHRISTIAN FINISHED the wall, tidied up the work area to make sure it would dry okay and there was nothing that might knock over or stain overnight, then went back to his room. It was indeed larger than Noah's, almost twice the size, and as a result it had been the recipient of the comfortable king-size bed that had arrived not long into Christian's time at the villa. The big guest room had actually received most of his attention, more than any other room in the house, because he knew it would be his living quarters for at least a couple of months. He might as well be comfortable.

He peeled off the cutoff jeans, themselves now soaked with sweat from the afternoon's labor, exposing himself to the closed room. Christian was no big believer in underwear, though he wondered if he should make an effort now that Noah was there.

Nah, he thought. The guy had said he didn't care. Besides, it wasn't like he'd be parading around in his birthday suit or anything. *Maybe if he seems uncomfortable.*

He showered, enjoying the cool water as it ran down his warm body. The walk-in wasn't as fancy as the one the Cunninghams wanted him to put in the master bathroom, but it sure felt great after a day of laboring in the heat. As he scrubbed paint off his skin, even scraping at some with his fingernails, he considered recommending some ceiling fans.

When he'd toweled off, he put on some cargo shorts and a loose-fitting white linen shirt and went looking for Noah.

"Something smells good," Christian remarked as he walked into the kitchen.

Noah, standing over a steaming sauté pan, smiled. "I found some chicken in the fridge, so I went with cacciatore," he said. "It was the first recipe I remembered off the top of my head."

"Smells amazing," Christian said, and Noah beamed.

"I need to grab a bottle of wine," he said, "to deglaze, simmer the chicken, and then serve. Can you watch the stove for a minute?"

Christian, who'd been leaning on the kitchen island munching a bell pepper, froze. "Uh… I meant it when I said that I'm really not a cook."

"Oh, c'mon," Noah teased. "Just keep an eye on the pan. If it stops misting and starts smoking, or if anything burns, turn the stove off. I'll be right back."

As Noah went down to the wine cellar, Christian took his place. He grabbed the cast iron pan, planning to shuffle the vegetables a little like he'd seen on cooking shows, but he got a shallow red burn on his skin for his trouble from the hot handle. Something that had been sizzling started making popping sounds, so he grabbed a towel and shook the pan again to try to undo whatever he'd done. The noise went away, and he breathed a sigh of relief.

"Do you have a preference?" Noah called up from the cellar.

"I like reds, but you're the expert," Christian said, inspecting his hand. It wasn't much of a burn, and he resolved not to let Noah see it. He didn't want the wine nerd thinking he was weak, after all, especially if they'd be spending another two months in the villa together.

"So do I," Noah's voice came bounding up the stairs, and soon the man himself came into view holding a bottle. "A nice Sangiovese, looks like it's from not too far away from here!"

Christian looked up at him and laughed.

"What?"

"Hold still, man."

Although somehow Noah hadn't realized it, he'd come up from the wine cellar with an enormous lump of spiderweb stuck in his hair. Christian walked across the kitchen toward him and began to disentangle it.

"Oh my God," Noah said, flustered when he saw the first clump. "That's disgusting!"

"It is actually kind of a lot, yeah," Christian agreed. "Hold still."

"Please tell me I didn't bring up the spider with it!"

"No, you're fine," Christian told him. He saw no signs of residency on the mop of Noah's blond hair. "It's a really old one, I can tell. Long since abandoned."

"Phew!" Noah said. "I mean, I'm not a wuss about spiders or anything, or else how would I expect to work in a wine cellar for a summer? I just don't like the idea of crawly things on my skin. You know what I mean?"

Christian, who could tell that Noah was obviously kind of a wuss about spiders, let him ramble on until he was comfortable again. He carefully picked each piece of web out of Noah's hair, unable as he was doing so to ignore the scent of Noah. It wasn't the man's conditioner, though he could smell that, nor any kind of cologne, not even any trace of body odor at the end of a long, hot day. Well, maybe a little of that.

It was the smell of Noah, the man, the guy who was standing less than four inches away from him. Christian wanted nothing more than to just wrap his arms around him and laugh about the spider's web. He knew better, though. Even if there wasn't the whole "pseudo-coworkers" aspect to their relationship, he couldn't afford to creep the guy out if they'd be living together for two months. So he resisted and sighed a little to himself.

"The veggies!" Noah suddenly cried, and Christian turned. There was definite smoke coming from the pan, so he ran his fingers through Noah's hair one last time before the wine nerd ran to save their dinner.

CHAPTER 5

NOAH HAD saved dinner, barely, pulling the veggies off the heat moments before any permanent damage was done. A little deglazing and sautéing later, and it was just right. He thought about asking Christian to set the table in the dining room, but when the bigger man sat down at the small wooden table in the kitchen, he thought better of it.

Rustic, he reminded himself. *Cozy.*

"Christian, I don't know where any of the dishes or things are," he said. "Can you get some plates, forks, glasses, that stuff?"

"Sure," Christian said and went rummaging through cabinets and drawers.

"Do you prefer Christian or Chris?" Noah asked.

"Either's fine," came the reply. "Most of my friends call me Chris, but my granddad and my... my parents, they usually say Christian."

"Do you mind if I call you Christian, then?" he asked. "If it's not too personal, I just like the sound of it."

"Not at all," the other man said, his voice much nearer than expected, causing Noah to wheel around and find Christian standing right next to him at the stove.

"Gah!" Noah said in surprise, dropping the wooden spoon into the pan.

Christian took a step back. "I'm sorry, did I surprise you? I'm— I'm sorry." He was holding two plates in one hand, and with the other, he began casually rubbing the back of his neck. "People say I sneak around sometimes, so I guess I'm just naturally quiet. I didn't mean to, like, creep on you or anything."

It was absolutely adorable, the way this big, muscled guy transformed into a kid at the junior high prom in the space of a second. *What a puppy dog*, Noah thought before he caught himself.

Noah gave an embarrassed laugh. "You're fine," he said. "It's cool. You just surprised me is all. Are those for the chicken?"

He pointed at the plates, and Christian handed them over. Noah served, and they both sat down to eat.

"So you said you're from Miami?" he asked.

Christian nodded, his mouth full of chicken, and spoke without swallowing. "Yeah, all my life. My grandparents brought my dad there when he was a baby, but they didn't really like it. So when my dad was out of college, they both moved back here. Dad stayed, met Mom and—"

The conversation was interrupted as they both watched a large piece of chicken, almost the size of a dime, fly out of Christian's mouth back onto the plate from which it had come.

"Dude," Noah said.

Christian laughed.

"Sorry," he said. "You probably think I'm, like, a pig or something. This is just so good! Really, man, this is amazing. You should be a chef."

He stuffed another forkful into his mouth and smiled as he chewed, his lips closed this time, and Noah laughed at last too.

"Thanks... I think," he said. "I thought in Europe when they like your food they burp, not spit it back up."

"Okay, hang on," Christian said. He picked up his wineglass and took a big drink.

"Oh please, no."

"One second." Christian thumped his chest a few times.

"You don't have to do this. In fact, please don't do this."

Christian smiled again, then opened his mouth, turned his head to one side so he was facing away from Noah, and ripped loose a belch that Noah was certain had come from some unknown pit in the other man's soul. It wasn't loud, but it was so deep that despite his disgust with the very childishness of it, Noah couldn't help but be impressed.

And when Christian smiled back at him once more, presumably for approval, Noah gave him the chuckle he seemed to need.

"Cool trick," he said. "You... a big drinker, then?"

Christian shrugged. "I guess, maybe, in college. Afterwards I tried to rein it in and all. All my friends are still big drinkers, but it's not healthy, and it's so expensive, y'know. All those reasons."

"It's Saturday," Noah said. "If you were home in Miami right now, what would you be doing?"

"Going out," Christian admitted. "Hitting a few bars. I mean, I'm not anti-drinking or anything. I just don't want to turn into one of those bar hounds by the time I'm thirty, know what I mean?"

Noah thought he did, but realized his impression from Ohio and New York might be different from one originating in Miami. In his waiter career, he'd seen lots of the type of guy Christian was describing, still the party animal way too long after the party had ended. Thirties sounded kind of young for that, though.

"What do you do back in the States?"

Christian gestured around the kitchen with his wineglass. "This. Lots of this. My dad's a lawyer, but he flips houses on the side, and I help him out, fixing them up. He jokes about how his father moved back to Italy to fix houses and he stayed in America to study law, but that he wound up in the family business anyway."

"Totally," Noah said. "So that's the new life plan? Flip houses? It's good money, isn't it?"

"Sure, I guess. But I don't know, I feel like I could do more. Isn't that the American dream? Grow up, do good in school, get a college degree, go do something with that degree, get the house with the fence and the dog, etc."

"What's your degree in?"

Christian winced. Noah wrinkled his brow in confusion.

"Communications," Christian told him. "Go ahead, laugh."

Noah's confusion continued. "Laugh at what?"

"Everybody does. The high school athlete who goes into communications in college, I've heard every joke."

"I don't know any jokes about communications," said Noah, who knew plenty of jokes about communications majors but opted to take a sip of wine instead of telling one.

Christian narrowed his eyes. "Oh come on. How it's such an easy major, how it doesn't really mean anything, all the rest. Very funny."

"I don't assume that," Noah said. "I bet it's not easier or harder than anything else. It all depends on your natural skills and how hard you work, right? It has to do with... public relations? Stuff like that?"

"Exactly!" Christian said, spearing another piece of chicken and stuffing it into his mouth. Noah couldn't ignore what sounded like several years of Christian defending his interests and maybe some pent-up rage.

"Was it... was it your parents that really didn't care for it?"

Christian, having gone before his eyes from childish glee to defensive male stereotype, went back to childish, but this time more morose. He shook his head. "My mom didn't, actually, but..."

He trailed off, and when he looked back up from his plate, he was smiling again. "Let's not talk about any of that, okay? What did you study? Are you still in school?"

"I AM," Noah said, scooping up a forkful of tomatoes. "Not undergrad, that's over with, but graduate school. At NYU."

Christian was impressed. *Here I was moaning about my parents and not making something of myself while this guy got into NYU's grad program.* He allowed himself a sigh of relief over not bringing up his parents' divorce. He'd almost said something, but it would've really soured the whole meal. Maybe even their whole working relationship, getting into something so personal when they'd just met.

"That's really cool. Studying what?"

"Art history," Noah replied. "Undergrad and graduate, both. That's kind of how I met the Cunninghams. One of my professors knows them and recommended me for any artwork they might need to have looked over in the villa. They told her that professionals had already appraised the works for insurance, that kind of thing, but they started talking about wine, and she brought up that I'm also studying to be a sommelier."

"That's... forgive me," Christian said. "That's a wine nerd, right? The guy at the fancy restaurant who knows all the wines?"

Noah laughed and took a sip of the Sangiovese. "Yeah, that's it."

"So wine's a hobby for you?"

"You bet," Noah said. "I enjoy it and I know a lot about it, so I guess you could call it a hobby. There's the money too, though."

Christian was surprised. "There's money in that?"

Noah grimaced. "There is... for waiters."

Christian laughed but stopped when Noah wasn't laughing.

"I'm a waiter, at a place in New York," he said. "I'm not ashamed of it, but I'm not, like, proud of it either. I like wine, and the best-paid waiter in the house is the one who knows all about the wines. So I got into this in order to be a better waiter, while I'm making ends meet trying to afford my New York City apartment on a grad student's stipend."

"No shame in that at all," Christian agreed. "It's a rough world. We've all got to make a living somehow. There's worse ways to put food on the table than waitin' 'em."

Noah smiled, one of those quiet little smiles that Christian had noticed were so much more subdued than his own. He could already tell that he was the more boisterous of the two, which suited him just fine.

As the meal wore on, they discussed school, food, politics, movies, and Christian was delighted to discover they had a lot of similar tastes. They both liked chicken but didn't like it fried, they both voted alike in the last few elections but agreed that discussing politics over dinner was a bad idea, and they both liked superhero movies but felt like the last few hadn't been as good. It pleased him to no end to find that the person he would be living with for a few months was someone he had things in common with.

Noah talked to him about wine, and Christian found it oddly much more fascinating than he ever had before. He quickly surmised that when he said he was studying to be a sommelier, Noah wasn't kidding around. He knew his years, his grape varietals, his sources and flavors.

"The big fancy master sommeliers have to take a test," he told Christian. "I mean, to get 'licensed' or 'official,' there are lots of tests, but the big one? Out of this world."

Christian, who'd never had much interest in tests (and wasn't good at passing them) nodded encouragingly to hear more.

"They bring you, blindfolded at first, into a dark room," Noah said, taking another sip from his glass, "and on a little table in front of you there are six glasses of wine, three whites and three reds. And you have to tell them all the information about the wine from look, taste, and smell alone."

"That sounds horrifying," Christian said.

Noah giggled but nodded. "I don't think I could ever do that. But knowing more is fun."

"I bet you could. You know way, way more than me!"

Noah laughed again, politely, but didn't reply.

It was well into the night when their bonding time was unceremoniously cut short by all the lights in the house going out at once. Across the table from him, Noah gave a little yelp, and suddenly Christian felt Noah's hand on his. Noah's skin was soft, he noticed, but his grip was firm. He embarrassed himself thinking about how nice it felt.

"What the hell?" Noah asked, sounding genuinely frightened.

"Don't worry about it." Christian tried to sound as reassuring as possible. "The fuses in this place are for crap so I have to keep replacing them. The electrician's coming out in a few days in case it's a wiring issue, but for now we get blowouts from time to time. Hang on a sec."

Christian got up, went to the drawer in the kitchen where he stored general handy items, and came back with a box of matches. He lit two candles in small metal holders from the kitchen sideboard and handed one to Noah. Its presence seemed to calm him, for which Christian was grateful.

"I have to go and—" He cut himself off and swore, then slapped his forehead.

"What is it?" Noah asked.

"I used my last replacement fuse the other day," he said. Christian had known he should go get more, right at the time, but he hadn't. "I'm afraid it's candles tonight. Is that okay with you?"

"Sure," Noah said. "Hey, I'm sorry if I... you know...."

"I do." Christian laughed. "And it's no big deal. A new place, a whole new country for you at least. A guy gets the jitters. I understand."

"Thanks. I guess we should call it a night."

Christian agreed and helped Noah clean up. They couldn't do all the washing up by candlelight, but they did what had to be done and left the rest for the morning. Together, trying to maximize the light from their candles, they walked out of the kitchen and down the hallway that connected the guest quarters.

"If you want to use my bathroom, go right ahead," Christian said in a low voice, not sure why he was whispering.

Noah made a face like he'd forgotten the bathroom situation and responded at the same volume. "If I just have to pee, is it really okay to do that in the... y'know, the toilet hole?"

"Sure," Christian said. "I swear that's getting installed real soon. The Cunninghams just wanted the fixtures to match, and they're not all ready. Only go number one, though."

"Oh, don't worry about that. Not a chance."

"Your shower works just fine," Christian whispered, "and there are a couple more candles in the closet if you need another."

Noah gave him a thumbs-up and went into the bedroom. "Good night," he said as he shut the door.

"Night," Christian replied.

He walked down the rest of the hall to his own larger bedroom and got ready for bed. When he was done with the bathroom and brushing his teeth, he slipped out of his clothes and climbed under the soft sheets into the big comfortable bed.

He thought about Noah. About how sweet he had turned out to be, how outgoing and friendly, what a good conversationalist. When Granddad had told him a wine snob was coming to live at the house and catalog the cellar, he'd expected someone older, or at least someone stuffier and uptight. Noah seemed like he could be a little uptight, he supposed, but not in a bad way.

Christian imagined Noah right then, getting ready for bed. Probably unpacking a few last things or double-checking to make sure he knew where the candles were in an emergency. He chuckled as he pictured Noah peeing into that hole in the tiled floor where a toilet soon would be, or undressing himself in the candlelit room.

As he pictured Noah undressing himself, the buttons coming undone one by one off that light yet still muscled chest, he felt a stirring within. When his imagination went further, picturing Noah slipping his shorts off and wondering what kind of underwear Noah wore, his hand slipped unbidden under the sheets in the direction of his crotch. What began there, as he fantasized about Noah in a variety of different underwear options, may have been involuntary, but it was far from unwanted. And it was certainly satisfying.

CHAPTER 6

OVER THE NEXT few weeks, the two settled into a routine. Noah learned that it was Christian's habit to rise earlier than he did, and he was touched to find that Christian used the time to assemble breakfast for the both of them. Occasionally Noah got up early enough to run into him and they might eat, but more often than not, he stayed up later and slept in later.

The meals Christian put together were simple, in keeping with his self-professed lack of skills in the kitchen, but Noah didn't mind. If he got out of bed and stumbled bleary-eyed to the little table where they'd first shared that chicken cacciatore and found a plate of overdone scrambled eggs and rapidly cooling bacon, he'd consider it a nice gesture all the same. Sometimes the meals would be even more bare than that, a bowl of cereal with a carafe of milk waiting to be poured, but as long as there was coffee, Noah was appreciative.

Always, whenever Noah arrived to find something waiting for him rather than the man himself, there was a little note. The first time, when he'd arrived to find a hardboiled egg and some sausage waiting, he'd taken it for the simple explanation that it obviously was: "Made extra for you, enjoy!" After several times, when the notes started saying things like "Hope you like granola!" or "I'll be cleaning the patio birdbath today :(" Noah found them endearing.

Without telling Christian, Noah saved every one.

After a quick shower and a pass through Christian's bathroom, Noah would start his day in earnest. If the Wi-Fi was working, and it almost always was after that first night, he'd check email and the various platforms of social media just in case the Cunninghams had sent him anything. It was rare but not unknown: Mr. Cunningham requesting a status update or Eloise writing him just to be encouraging. Noah kept them both apprised and got on with his real job.

Most of the day was spent in the cellar. The wine cellar was an enormous task, a fact that hit him every time he went down there. Finishing the work of cataloging it within two months still seemed feasible to him, but it was a full-time job.

For every single bottle, he considered it his duty to discover its origin as best he could, determine its commercial value, and (operating under the assumption the Cunninghams intended to keep it rather than sell it) write any notes about its proper storage and care. Some needed to be kept away from light sources, some needed to be turned more often than others, etc.

He always brought his laptop with him, and the internet made the job a lot easier than it could've been. This fact was not lost on him, though he had also brought from home a number of small wooden boxes that held blank index cards. Sometimes they were easier to organize in a hurry than the database was. With recent vintages that still had their full labels on them, he could crack through them in record time. It was the older, more curious bottles that demanded his attention, and those were many.

He found it pleasant work. While the rest of the villa suffered the heat of the summer Tuscany sunshine, the cellar was always the same: cool and a little damp. Electric lighting ran overhead, which at some point someone had installed in order to modernize past the now-empty wall sconces hung about head-height on all the walls, and the fact that it was always the same light, the same temperature, the same humidity meant it was easy to lose track of time.

Noah would take little breaks, and each one would be spent wondering what Christian was up to. It was a big house, but they did bump into each other from time to time, usually when Noah went up for air, or for lunch or a snack. Christian, often carrying something heavy or cleaning something disgusting, was always polite and kind and seemed happy to see him. Noah tried to return the favor, imagining that his little breaks were pleasant for Christian too.

THE MOMENTS when he and Noah just happened to run into each other, as they both did their very different work in very different parts of the house, were the best parts of Christian's day. He started to look forward to them, and eventually to find ways to encourage them.

The wine cellar was the absolute least of Christian's problems. It was on the long-term to-do list that he and an electrician might modernize the lighting and install a few temperature and humidity controls, but the cavern was a perfect natural spot, and everyone involved knew it. The Cunninghams had made clear to Silvio, Christian's grandfather, who had in turn made clear to Christian, that the cellar was not a construction priority.

The plumbing, however, was very high on the to-do list. It was archaic, and while he had been known to dabble in light repairs or even installations, he was no certified plumber. The problem of finding one was compounded by an old Italian feud, of all things, a fact that almost literally drove Christian up the wall. The only plumber in the village nearby was very skilled, and his operation definitely could've handled the work, but his grandfather had insulted Silvio's father or married some member of the family he shouldn't have (Christian wasn't clear on the details). For whatever reason, Christian's grandfather had the final say on what contractors would be hired, and he refused to give the man's company a lucrative contract. For his part, the plumber refused to ever work with a Caravelli anyway, no matter the money involved.

Which left Christian looking for the next nearest plumber who could handle a job like the villa. Balancing those two criteria was difficult. Plenty of plumbers had companies nearby that were too small to use. (This was not a "one man and his son" operation.) Larger firms that could send a big enough team were farther away ,a factor sure to be included in their bid.

And there was also the electrical to consider.

These were the thoughts going through Christian's head as he worked under the kitchen sink for what felt like the thousandth time. Every time he sorted out one of the house's many plumbing problems, another reared its head, sometimes one that he thought he had fixed before. When Noah had informed him that there was no water coming from the kitchen faucet, he had thrown up his hands in frustration and gotten to work.

"I… am not… a damn… plumber!" he growled, grinding his teeth as he twisted the pipe under the sink tighter and tighter. When he'd complained to his grandfather about how much work he was doing, not only work that he wasn't qualified to do but frankly work that was a lot harder than he'd thought he'd be doing, the old man had just handed him a big wrench and told him to be grateful he wasn't getting smacked with it instead.

Sweaty, bruised from having lain down on what turned out to be a lug nut in order to work on the sink from underneath, Christian finally crawled out from under it and turned on the faucet. There was a grumbling sound, followed by brown water. Christian raised the large metal wrench high above his head and began cursing, running a blue streak through his English expletive vocabulary before deciding that an Italian sink probably needed to be cursed at in Italian.

His vocabulary was more limited there, and the sink didn't appreciate it either way. With a sigh he crawled back under the sink.

It was late in the afternoon when he finally got the water flowing properly again. There had been more cursing, naturally, but Christian believed that the sink had come to fear and respect him as much as he did it in return.

"Don't make me have to have this conversation again," he said, holding the wrench out menacingly.

The sink, pouring out crystal clear water, hiccupped once but otherwise didn't react.

Little chores like that, though uncomfortably common, weren't the sum total of his days. He spent plenty of time juggling multiple responsibilities, replying to email after email from prospective contractors, even managing his grandfather's expectations. These were things his life before manual labor under the Italian sun had prepared him for, and he found some satisfaction in the sense of accomplishment they gave him. Simple things like painting, refurbishing some of the original furniture, replacing bits of wood here or there, were all well within his skills and got him away from the laptop he used to manage the rest of the project.

They also meant he got to see Noah more often, which was a pleasant little joy in and of itself.

Christian had noticed the wine nerd liked to sleep in later than he did, and that suited him fine. He made breakfasts and left the leftovers behind, often with a cute little note, before he got started on the business of refurbishment. In his imagination, just as a game to play throughout the day, he pictured Noah finding the notes and keeping them. It obviously wasn't true, because Noah never said anything about them, but Christian figured a fun little fantasy wasn't doing anyone any harm.

Their schedules rarely lined up for lunch, but dinner together became a regular thing. They got to know each other better. Christian found every detail of Noah's life, so different from his own, absolutely fascinating. Christian had done a number of different sports in high school, like cross-country and lacrosse but never football, which just didn't suit him right. Noah, on the other hand, had spent a miserable month on the swim team before quitting and focusing on his schoolwork.

"I never would've guessed it," Christian said one night over some spaghetti carbonara and a dry Cabernet. "I mean… you look fit, dude. Seriously. Tight."

Noah blushed. "Well thank you, and I definitely kept swimming. Just not on the team."

"Not into team sports so much?"

"Not really, but it was more than that. It was, like, a perfect storm of reasons to walk away. The guys on the team were really clique-y, they'd all known each other since grade school, and the coach was just the worst. One of those guys with no interest in the team, y'know? Just there because he'd won a bunch of trophies a decade ago and no one at the school had the guts to fire him."

Christian nodded. He definitely knew the type.

"But I loved swimming," Noah went on, pausing for a sip of his wine. "The cool water on your skin, the silence underneath. Those Speedos… oops!"

Noah giggled, and Christian guessed he was just a little bit drunk. He smiled, hoping he could somehow signal with his eyes, his face, his body language that he didn't care. That Noah could be safe around him.

"I didn't mean to say that," Noah said, "but I guess I had a little more of this bottle than you did." Still smiling beneath flushed cheeks, he picked up the bottle and inspected it. He looked like he figured out what Christian already knew: that it was almost empty and Christian had only had one glass.

"It's okay, man, I know what you mean," Christian replied. He picked up his own glass and drained it. "Those tight little swim trunks… damn, do I know what you mean!"

Noah smiled at him again, and Christian wasn't sure what he saw in that smile. Uncertainty? Bonhomie? Dare he hope… flirtation?

"Anyway, I kept swimming," Noah said, "because I liked it. I still do, when I can."

Suddenly Christian was very conscious of the pool outside and how unusable it was at the moment. A thing like that had to be very tempting to Noah, but disheartening too because it was so full of muck and algae that he couldn't possibly just jump in.

"Well," he said, "it might make you happy to know that I think I finally found a plumber."

"Oh?"

Christian had not, in fact, settled on a plumber, but he was getting close, so he continued. "He has a pool guy, so we might be able to get that thing out there up and running pretty soon. Just, if you wanted to swim from time to time."

Noah brightened, then pursed his lips and shrugged. "I didn't pack a swimsuit."

"What?" Christian blurted out with mock surprise that made Noah laugh again. "You came all the way from New York to Italy to spend the summer and you didn't even pack a suit?"

Noah shook his head. "My grad student eyes were dancing with visions of Merlot and dollar signs, what can I say."

"I can probably find you one," Christian said. "Or if not, well, you know... I won't look."

He winked. Noah blushed even redder.

"On that note," said the tipsy, almost-inebriated, Noah, "I think we better clear this table. I don't know about you, but I'm calling it a night."

Until he drifted off to sleep, Christian didn't stop thinking about the fact that Noah hadn't explicitly said no.

CHAPTER 7

NOAH AWOKE the next morning to a harsh reminder that "wine drunk" is not a good way to start the day. He wasn't sure what he'd said to Christian, but he was certain that he'd thoroughly embarrassed himself. Christian, who had been nothing but kind to him, who had welcomed him into their mutual Tuscan villa endeavor like he was a long-lost family member. He resolved to himself that in the future, one glass of wine with dinner was more than adequate.

Still clad only in his white-and-blue striped boxer shorts, he made for the bathroom, relieved himself, and then slipped them off to step in the shower. To his surprise, however, the handles didn't produce water. He tried turning just the hot, then just the cold, then turning both at the same time, then turning them all the way or just a little bit at a time, but nothing worked. The most he got when he turned both on full blast was a rumbling, gurgling sound deep in the pipes that scared the hell out of him, so he quickly shut them off.

Maybe Christian has water, he thought. *Maybe it's just my shower.*

He pulled his underwear back on, adding a blue T-shirt for modesty's sake, slipped on his flip-flops, and headed down the hall. At the end of it, he knocked on Christian's door.

"Hey, Christian?" he called. "Can I come in? My shower's not working."

There was no reply, so Noah tried the handle. The door opened easily, and he poked his head inside.

Christian wasn't present as far as Noah could see, and he thought for a moment about whether he should go in. On the one hand, he wasn't the type of person to invade another's personal space. If he'd found Christian just casually wandering through his own bathroom, he'd be upset. On the other hand, Christian had been very open and welcoming for Noah's entire stay so far. He hadn't checked the time, but it was late enough into the morning that Christian was probably already active in some other part of the house. And he had said Noah could use that bathroom whenever he wanted.

As he quibbled with himself, he detected an odd scent, something masculine but... off. He realized it was coming from him: his own body odor had turned on him. He blamed a sweaty night in the Tuscan heat, as well as his pores trying to eliminate more alcohol than they were accustomed to.

That settled it. He had to shower, and he had to do it right away. If Christian's shower was working, then Noah was jumping right in.

He entered the room and, tiptoeing on instinct as if he were committing a crime of some sort, crept up to the bathroom. The door was open a crack, which further confirmed to Noah that Christian wasn't around. Who would leave their bathroom door open while they were using it?

He stepped up to the door and pushed it open, then immediately discovered who would leave their bathroom door open while they were using it: Christian Caravelli.

The tanned Miami Italian with a body to die for stood before him, wearing only a towel... that was wrapped around his head. He was drying his hair, his eyes covered, humming to himself.

Mortified, Noah covered his mouth before he could make a sound. The bathroom was still steamy so Christian had clearly been in the shower only moments before Noah knocked. Droplets of water that clung to his perfect chest and his strong arms confirmed the theory. Noah's brain told him to run like hell, to get away as fast as he could before he ruined the friendly relationship he'd built with the other man. But every other part of him, like the pounding in his chest and the stirring in his loins, urged him to stay.

43

Christian's body was everything Noah had pictured it would be, and more. The thick pecs he'd become accustomed to seeing, with their dark brown nipples, glistened in the lights of the vanity nearby. He could make out the ripple of the muscles in the other man's arms as he vigorously shook the towel through the dark brown hair that Noah knew lay underneath. The patches of hair below Christian's armpits were brown also, curly and coiling as they clung to the still-wet places of him there.

Below those pecs he knew so well from everyday exposure, below the abs that he saw more often than he'd dreamed he would when he first agreed to spend a summer in Tuscany, below the perfect *V* line that he'd seen hints of from time to time leading out of Christian's favorite cutoff jean shorts, was Christian's cock. And it too was magnificent. Noah found himself enraptured, unwilling to take his eyes off it. Christian was uncircumcised, unlike Noah, and the foreskin of that beautiful appendage came to a point just past the tip. Noah, who'd only been with one uncut guy before, felt like it was daring him to roll it back and claim the treasure within. The balls, so warm and wet from the shower, hung low in their sac behind the cock but didn't quite reach below the tip. Low as they were, Christian's cock was longer. Slender compared to some that Noah had seen, but just as inviting.

Above the Caravelli family treasures sat a mass of dark brown curls, wet from the shower and matted against the skin. Noah had no doubt that Christian trimmed his pubic hair and wondered what the full effect of the sculpting would look like when the man was totally dry. A teasing of hair, thicker than what was on his chest but thinner than the bush below, formed an inviting treasure trail between the two.

"Well good morning to you too."

Christian's voice broke the spell, and Noah looked up. The white cotton bath towel that had been wrapped around the handyman's head was now hanging around his neck. Christian was smiling at him.

Noah blushed so quickly he could feel it bloom across his cheeks. "Oh my God, dude, I am so, so sorry."

Christian shrugged. "Good morning all around, that is," he said, and gestured his head downward.

Noah looked down at himself, still wearing only boxers and a T-shirt, and saw the obvious tent that had grown in his shorts when he wasn't paying attention. Or rather, when his mind was elsewhere.

Embarrassed beyond what he'd previously thought physically possible, Noah reached down and clutched his own erect penis in order to cover himself.

"I am… I'm so sorry," he said. "First I got drunk last night and I don't know what I said, and then you find me in here like this. I swear there's an explanation."

Christian, standing nude with a towel wrapped around his neck and holding the ends of it with both hands, waited with a faint smile on his lips. "And that would be…?"

"My shower's not working," Noah replied. "The knobs aren't doing anything, except when I had them both on all the way, there was this weird kind of rumbling sound, so I came in here to see if yours was working and if I could borrow it because I stink, then I knocked on your door, but I guess you didn't hear me, so I came in because you said I could whenever I needed to, and then I pushed open your door because it didn't occur to me that someone who was using their bathroom might leave the door open while they were doing that and—"

"Noah, breathe," Christian said.

Noah slumped against the doorframe and gasped for air. He'd recounted the whole mortifying tale but still hadn't been able to take his eyes off Christian's cock. His one genuine attempt to be a good guy rather than a creep and look somewhere else had been a brief second of looking at the mirror, which he quickly discovered had an ideal view of Christian's perfectly rounded ass.

As if sensing his discomfort, Christian pulled the towel off his neck and wrapped it around his waist. As much as a prurient, secret part of him had enjoyed the view and would treasure it always, Noah was grateful that he did.

"I'm comfortable with my body, Noah," Christian said. "I was raised in… an understanding environment. If you're not comfortable with it, then I'm sorry if I caused you that discomfort."

"No, I'm sorry. Really. This room is your space. It was wrong of me to just intrude. You should feel safe to be just as naked as you want to in here."

Christian laughed. "Permission appreciated."

"Oh no, I didn't mean—"

"I'm teasing you."

"Oh."

"Since it obviously makes you uncomfortable," Christian continued before looking down at where Noah's hands were still clasped, "or at least it makes most of you uncomfortable, then let's just agree that in here I might be naked sometimes. And if you come in here, you might see naked Christian. Is that fair?"

He reached out a hand to shake, which Noah took.

"More than fair. Yes. Totally. And once again, I'm sorry."

"Nothing to be sorry about. I'm gonna go to my room and finish drying off. You grab your towel or whatever and feel free to use my shower, all right?"

Noah nodded. "Thanks."

WHEN NOAH pulled his hand away, Christian saw out of the corner of his eye a glimpse of pale pink skin through the opening of the boxers. He forced himself not to break eye contact with Noah as they finished their exchange and Noah went off to find his towel.

He stepped out into the bedroom, dried himself as quickly as he could, and made sure to have the towel wrapped once more around his waist by the time Noah got back. When he did, he smiled, waved a little awkwardly, and went into the bathroom. He was still wearing the same blue T-shirt but had his own towel wrapped around his own waist.

Because he doesn't want to wear any more clothes to the shower than he needs? Christian wondered. *Or because he's still hiding an erection he doesn't want me to see?*

Christian couldn't be sure, though of course he knew which answer he preferred, but as Noah shut the bathroom door, he couldn't help but see another flash of skin out of the corner of his eye, reflected in the mirror. He wasn't certain, but it seemed like Noah had been wearing nothing under the towel.

Whether it was his imagination that filled in the blanks and yielded a perfect round bubble butt or whether that ass had actually been there, Christian had only his hopes.

He dressed, deciding to wear a white sleeveless T-shirt above his cutoffs if only in an effort to emphasize to Noah that he understood the wine nerd's discomfort. Besides, if all went according to plan, he'd be going out to meet with a plumbing contractor. Christian was running late that morning because he'd been answering emails, and one particular plumbing company that he thought looked just perfect had sent him a perfectly acceptable bid. With that in mind, he put on socks and work boots rather than his regular leather thong sandals.

Just in time, too, he thought. *If Noah's shower is going to need work all of a sudden.*

He didn't see Noah again until that evening, though he left the usual breakfast. He meandered around the house for a few hours, fixing this thing or that while he waited to head down to the village. Noah, as far as he knew, went straight down to the wine cellar. When the time came, Christian hopped on his bike, rode down to the village where his grandfather was waiting to loan him the old beater that he called a car, and headed for the next town over.

The meeting went well, unbelievably well. Christian was proud of himself, and proud of the way he had argued on his grandfather's behalf. He'd impressed the representative with his knowledge of the building and its needs, he asked all the right questions so there could be no doubt he was a savvy customer, and he even got the company to knock a few euros off the bid when he convinced them that some add-ons were unnecessary. Best of all, another job had recently cancelled and they'd be able to start the next day. All in all, it was a most productive afternoon.

When he dropped the car off back at his grandfather's, the old man insisted he come in and sit for a while. Christian, despite his belief that he had better things to do, did as he was told. Silvio probably just wanted an update on the progress. He had an email address to which Christian had been sending updates but he knew his grandfather probably hadn't read any of them. The villa, however, turned out not to be the only thing on his mind.

"Christian!" his grandfather cried when he returned, standing on his bad leg to embrace him as if they hadn't seen each other just a few hours ago. "Tell me how it went."

They both sat down on the porch at a small wooden table that the elder Caravelli had built decades before, and Christian dutifully filled his grandfather in on the details of the contract he'd just signed with the nearby plumbing company. Right away it was clear that the old man wasn't really interested. He nodded a few times, clapped his grandson on the back once or twice when Christian told him how he'd maneuvered the negotiations, and soon changed the subject when all the relevant details were done.

"Tell me," Silvio finally said. "Tell me all about this man that is living up at the villa with you, the wine expert. He's not unpleasant, is he?"

"No, Granddad, he's nice," Christian replied. "His name is Noah, and it's fine. He works in the wine cellar, and I work on the house."

"And he is always in the wine cellar?" his grandfather asked.

"Well no, not always. He doesn't sleep there."

The old man pursed his lips as if he disapproved, but his bad leg kept him from smacking Christian in the back of the head.

"We bump into each other," Christian went on, the awkward but salacious encounter from that morning floating to the top of his mind. "We have dinner together. He's a decent guy."

Silvio's eyebrows went up, and a sly smile crossed the man's lips.

"What?"

"Dinner?" he inquired innocently. "You have dinner together with this man?"

"Granddad." Christian rolled his eyes. "It's not like that."

"Why? He is old?"

"No, he's about my age."

"He's unsightly? A hunchback?"

"Granddad! We don't use that word!"

The old man put up both hands. "Apologies. Please apologize to the hideous Noah for me."

"He's not hideous at all, Granddad," Christian said. "In fact… he's kind of attractive."

"Oh, now I understand," Silvio said with a wink.

"Granddad."

"What?" He threw both hands up in the air. "What do you want from me? My grandson is having dinner every night for two weeks with a handsome young man who knows wine. Is that not a reason for me to be happy? Shall I assume, from what I know of you, that he also cooks these dinners?"

Christian narrowed his eyes at his grandfather and refused to dignify that with a response. His grandfather laughed.

"Granddad," Christian said with a sigh, "it's not like that. Really it isn't. It can't be, it shouldn't be."

"And why not? He is not… you know?"

"Oh, he is," Christian admitted, thinking back to Noah's *in vino veritas* moment from the previous night. "But we work together. We're going to be living together for at least six more weeks. What if I make a move and he's not interested? Or he is interested, but it goes south somehow? We'd be stuck together in that house for the rest of the summer, possibly driving each other crazy!"

The old man reached across the table and took Christian's hand in his. Christian loved his grandfather's hands. His memories of them stretched back to when he was just a small boy visiting Italy with his parents. Those hands had been so big, gnarled but powerful, wrapping easily around his own. Now Christian, so much older, had hands that the older man's couldn't quite encircle, and though they were still strong enough to earn a hard workman's living, Silvio's hands had become wrinkled and the skin a little thinner. Still, he held his grandson's hand.

"My boy," he said, "in this life you will come close to beauty, and to romance, many, many times. Take it from me. When you are old, sitting at a table that you built yourself and watching the sun go down, both over the valley and in your own life, it will be the romances you did not take that you will regret. Not the times you tried and failed."

Christian sighed. It was a speech he'd heard before, from his parents, in movies, on greeting cards probably, but when he thought of Noah, it seemed to mean something different to him all of a sudden.

"Measure your life by the hearts you have held with yours," Silvio told him. "Not by the butts you failed to fuck."

"Granddad!"

The old man laughed.

CHAPTER 8

IT WAS after dark when Christian got home. Noah had spent the day feeling nervous, wondering whether Christian was intentionally avoiding him, despite the note bearing a smiley face that had been sitting next to a light fruit salad that morning.

He'd tried to focus on work, but to no avail. Thoughts of the morning encounter filled his mind. How awkward and flustered he had been, how cool and collected Christian had been, both just mortified him. He recounted the events over and over again.

Of course, when finally forced to admit it to himself, his embarrassment wasn't the only reason he went over what had happened more than once. Dear God, where had bodies like that been all his life? Noah had never considered himself a "nerd,"—he was academically inclined but he kept himself in good shape. Was this what he'd been missing by not dating jocks? His mind raced back to a few odd matchups that could've been improved if he'd been a little more open-minded.

Eventually, seated in the wine cellar with his laptop on his knees, not to mention an erection that simply would not be ignored, Noah decided he had to do something about it.

"I'll just tell him I find him attractive," he said aloud to the empty cavern. "What could possibly go wrong?"

Instantly, of course, about a hundred things ran through his mind.

There was the coworkers aspect, the roommates aspect... and it occurred to him that having seen Christian naked would only make things worse! No matter how comfortable with his body he might be—and Noah took him at his word when he said he was—once Noah's interest in him was on the table, there'd be no taking it back.

51

He'd put Noah's wandering eyes into context, their proper context, and everything could change. He might start to question whether Noah had meant to walk in on him like that, whether he was living at the villa with some New York City pervert who got off on spying on people!

Could he have me arrested? Noah wondered. He doubted it, if only because it truly had been an accident and he could say that as a defense, but also because Christian didn't seem like the type. *If he got that upset about it, he'd probably just punch my lights out!*

There was, of course, the slim chance that Christian would be flattered… maybe even interested. Noah pushed that scenario out of his mind.

"Better to keep my mouth shut," he said glumly. He turned back to the wine database he was building and tried to put thoughts of Christian (clothed and otherwise) to rest.

When he noticed the time on his laptop's clock he saved, folded it up, and went to the rack of wines that the Cunninghams had said he and Christian could use. The woman who dropped off their food had included some ribeye steaks he had been eyeing, and before he went up the stairs, he grabbed a nice Barolo to complement them. In the kitchen he seasoned the two steaks with nothing more than heavy salt and fresh black pepper, then set them aside so the pan would have time to heat up. When they were cooked, along with some fresh vegetables for the side, he set them out, poured the wine, and did no more than nibble as he waited.

By the time the sun had set for real, Noah decided that Christian wasn't coming. Sitting at the small table, missing the casual intimacy of his regular dinner companion, Noah felt really and truly stung. Obviously no matter what he had said, Christian had been offended. Noah was just about to start really eating his steak instead of just picking at it when he heard the front door close.

"Hello?" called a familiar voice.

"In here!" Noah shouted. His heart beat faster, and he felt his cheeks flush. He couldn't contain his excitement at the possibility that it had all been a misunderstanding after all.

"What smells so good?" Christian called from the entryway.

"Steaks," Noah yelled back, "and a nice red."

"Yum!" Christian said as he walked through the kitchen door. He was smiling, still wearing a sleeveless T-shirt and his jean shorts, and the smile got brighter when his eyes met Noah's. "That sounds delicious, thanks!"

"They might be a little cold by now."

Christian walked up behind Noah, reached his arm around the man's shoulder, and held a hand close to the slab of meat on the plate. He was so close, the gesture so intimate, it almost took Noah's breath away. Noah could smell him, the sweat of having been running around all day, and hear him as he panted low breath after breath.

He turned, and Christian's face was at his. Almost kissing distance.

"I can still feel some heat," Christian said.

Noah cleared his throat, gestured across the table, and Christian sat. They began to dig in.

"Sorry I'm so late," Christian said, "but I come bearing good news! I found a plumbing company and signed a contract. They'll start work tomorrow."

The idea of a cool shower every morning against the summer heat, not to mention having his own toilet, brought a fresh smile to Noah's lips. "That's fantastic! I'm glad to hear it."

Christian nodded, then swallowed a bite of steak with a splash of wine. "Thought you would be. I told them to be prepared to start in your bathroom, as long as that's okay with you."

"No need." Noah waved him off. "I mean, it's the Cunninghams' house. Surely their bathroom needs to be finished up first, right?"

"Why?" Christian took another swig from his wineglass. "They're not going to be here for months, long after you and I are gone, but you and me, we're here right now. May as well make the place livable for us first. So they'll work on your bathroom first. And then the pool."

Christian's wisdom made sense to Noah, tainted slightly by his selfish hopes for indoor plumbing, so he nodded assent and let it go.

"I have to admit," he finally volunteered, "I was… I was a little worried you were avoiding me."

"Why?" Christian asked, his face total innocence.

"You know… because of what happened this morning."

"Oh, that!" Christian laughed again, that soft endearing sound halfway between a chuckle and a bellow. "Noah, I meant what I said. I don't care. Neither should you."

Once again Noah allowed himself to relax. "Thanks, Christian, thanks again, I mean. It's not that I'm, like, uptight about it or anything."

"Never thought you were."

Christian held up one hand and inspected it. From across the table, Noah watched Christian take in the sight of steak juices running down his left thumb. Then he watched Christian nonchalantly put that thumb into his mouth and suck, deeply sucking and slurping on it to get the juices off.

Once again, Noah was no longer relaxed.

GOD DAMN it, Christian thought as he tongued the last juices off his skin. *He really must not be interested after all. Am I being too subtle?*

He'd violated Noah's personal space and delivered his cheesy line about "feeling the heat," he'd told Noah about the plumbers, a gesture that he thought would've shown that he cared, and now he was performing fellatio on his own thumb.

No guy that Christian had ever been with had played harder to get than that.

I guess he's not playing, Christian finally decided, and his spirits sank a bit. He'd taken his grandfather's advice to heart and come home determined to make a move, but he'd seen how uncomfortable his nudity had made Noah. Pouncing on him and ravishing him until they both saw stars wasn't an option. Having tried finesse, and finesse having failed him, Christian decided one more time to let it go. If there was to be a first move, it would be Noah's.

"This steak is really, really good," he said, and he meant it. To complement his new "fuck it" attitude, he washed down his glass of wine and poured a second. He held the bottle out to Noah, who seemed to consider it for a moment but ultimately smiled and nodded. Christian topped off both glasses.

"So that was my day. How did things go for you down in the catacombs?"

"Oh, fine. Another day in the dark and damp."

"I'll say. You should think about getting some sun." Christian gestured at Noah with his fork. "Maybe pale is in where you're at, but if you get home from your vacation without a tan, none of your friends are going to believe you really went to Italy."

Noah laughed. "Oh, they know. I only have a few close friends, but they know where I'm at."

"Bet they're all jealous."

"A bit." Noah's smirk made it sound like he was thinking of someone in particular, and Christian smiled too.

"Well then think of my national pride!" he exclaimed. He held his glass up for inspection. "You went to Italy, and all you brought back was a paycheck and some memories of great wine? Hardly!"

They both laughed at the joke, and Christian thought he saw Noah relax again as dinner went on. They talked about friends back in the States, and he surprised Noah when he said that he too didn't really have that many.

"I'd have thought you'd have been the rock star," Noah admitted.

"Not *close* friends, I mean," Christian clarified. "There's a crowd I go out with on weekends, but it's not the same."

"Where in Miami do you live?" Noah asked. "Right in the heart of party central, I bet?"

Christian made a face. "Actually...."

Noah cocked an eyebrow.

"I live with my parents."

"So? No shame in that," Noah said, gulping the last of his second glass. "A lot of our generation do. The economy and all that."

"It's... it's different," Christian admitted.

As he pictured his family home, he suddenly realized there were tears forming at the corners of his eyes. He wasn't sure why he felt so emotional all of a sudden. Maybe it was the wine, maybe it was his granddad's comments earlier, or maybe it was just Noah's comforting presence making it feel safe to open up a little.

Noah reached across the table. He took Christian's hand, the same hand his grandfather had taken just a few hours before. Where the old man's hand had felt wrinkled, Noah's skin was smooth, but that reassuring strength was still there. Silvio's hand had the strength of a man who'd worked a solid day's work every day of his life. Noah's was different, a strength buried deep inside, as if there were a core of iron unshakable within.

"You don't have to talk to me about it if you don't want to but... what's the matter, man? Christian?"

"It's... they're—" he stammered. "It's my folks. I'm here this summer because they're talking about getting a divorce."

Noah didn't take his hand away. "I'm sorry to hear it. Really."

Christian felt foolish, his eyes brimming with tears, but he refused to let them spill over. "I feel so stupid about it. Crying like a little kid. I'm an adult. They're adults. It's not like I'm eight years old."

"I get it," Noah said. "It's still a big change for you, life-altering. Especially since you live with them."

"To be honest, I've been thinking about not going back."

Noah's eyebrows went up. "To the US?"

Christian nodded. "I mean, what's there for me to go back to? Mom and Dad, who fight like cats and dogs? A bunch of so-called friends who won't miss me? A degree that's taking me nowhere and no prospects for the future?"

He gestured around the house. "At least here, with Granddad, there's something. The name Caravelli is worth something in this part of Italy, it means a hard worker and reliable skills. What's more, I learned today that I'm actually good at this. Granddad's getting older. I could take over the family business."

Noah nodded slowly. "I mean, sure, if that's what you want. It sounds like a great opportunity when you put it like that."

He wasn't sure why, but Christian felt like Noah sounded uncertain somehow. Was it wishful thinking, or did the idea of Christian staying on in Italy when Noah went home rub him the wrong way?

Noah got up from his chair, came around to Christian's side of the table, and hugged him. It caught Christian off guard, such a close physical gesture when he was used to Noah being so distant. There was support and friendship emanating from the strength in Noah's arms, but nothing intimate. Just an expression of this odd friendship that the two men, unlike each other in so many ways, had built. Christian returned it, and after a moment they let go.

"Thanks, man, really," he said. "Thanks for letting me whinge about my life."

Noah gripped him by the shoulder with a smile and then returned to his seat to finish the meal. "We all need a shoulder sometimes, nothing strange about it."

"It still feels silly to complain. Parents with money, friends waiting for me in Miami, and a job in Italy, and here I am whining about the one or two little things that aren't perfect."

"It's subjective," Noah said around a mouthful of steak. "Who am I to say your pain's less than mine just because our circumstances are different?"

"Thanks just the same."

CHAPTER 9

NOAH WAS in the wine cellar working when the plumbing contractors arrived. Christian asked him to come up and say hello, just so he wouldn't see them and think there were burglars (or vice versa), and he did. None of them spoke English, and Noah's Italian was passable at best, so the conversation was limited to a friendly wave on either side. The trouble started almost immediately as soon as he went back down.

First came the noise. It became clear over the next few days that the villa actually needed some pretty significant plumbing work, in the sense that floors would be ripped up in a few places. An electrician was brought in to see if they could work side by side, rather than risk tearing up anything more than necessary, and while the men agreed that it was possible, it meant that even more of the house was suddenly under construction.

What had been Christian's one-man effort to paint and replace some wood had become what Noah had always known it eventually would be: he was living in a construction site.

He had to learn to get up very, very early, which disagreed with him in every way. After an incident where one of the workmen came into Christian's bathroom to use the toilet while Noah was still using Christian's shower, however, there was no alternative. The workers had no respect for personal space, so he had to retreat.

Because Christian had made his guest bedroom a priority, for which Noah was grateful, it even meant that his own room offered little relief. Only in the evening when the workmen had gone would it finally be empty, by which time he was usually making dinner for the two of them. The result was that only after dinner would he finally get a chance to inspect how much of a mess they had left behind. When the new plumbing was installed, the old plumbing fixed as needed, and a toilet finally, blessedly, put into place, he discovered that because they'd become accustomed to working out of his room, the workmen had decided to keep using it for the doors that accessed the pool!

The wine cellar became his escape, the one place where he could be assured of peace and quiet. While the occasional rumble or crash still sounded ominously from above, the insulation in the cavern was ideal. An electrician came down once to do a preliminary inspection of the lighting, just to get an idea of how big that job would be if it ever came up (or so Noah thought he said), but otherwise it was a cool, blissful oasis from the chaos upstairs.

At dinner one night over some hearty sandwiches and a nice young Chianti, he asked Christian if he had any idea how much longer the construction would be going on.

"I mean, I know it's a renovation," Noah said. "I'm not complaining or anything. I get that it's a big job. Mostly I just want to know how much longer they're going to be occupying my room."

Christian laughed at Noah's self-deprecating joke, for which Noah was glad.

"Well, I'm sorry to say it, but it's going to be another few weeks at least," Christian said, ripping the bad news off like a bandage.

Noah stopped smiling. "I won't lie, Christian, that's not exactly what I wanted to hear."

"What can I do? The plumbing work is extensive and the electrical is… less so, but it's still complicated. Unfortunately, some pretty major junctions run under your bedroom. I'm sorry."

Noah rolled his eyes in a large, dramatic fashion, hoping Christian would see it was a joke, and he must've, because he laughed again. "Fine. Can I switch bedrooms, then? There are two other guest rooms, right?"

"If you want to," Christian said. "But the situation there isn't much better than it was when you first got here. I've cleaned up a little, but they haven't been my main focus. Besides which, the crew is going to have to get into those sooner or later as well. The only rooms that are really well done, they told me, are the master bedroom and—"

"And your room," Noah finished for him. Christian nodded, his lips pursed and twisted to one side as if he regretted having to say it.

"And I'm sorry, but I don't want anyone in the master bedroom that doesn't have to be there. I put a lot of work into it before you got here, and I have it just perfect. Unless the contractors need to get into it to do something, I can't just open it up."

"Can I hang out in your room, then?" Noah asked.

Christian hesitated.

"I can sleep in my room," Noah said. "I don't mind cleaning everything off when they're done for the day, not if it means having my own bed every night. But there's no place in this house that's off-limits to them. Nowhere but the wine cellar, which I admit is nice for me, the master bedroom, and—"

"And my room," Christian finished, echoing Noah's earlier statement. "Sure. I'd hate to think of you hiding out in that damp cellar just to get away from the noise and stuff. If you need somewhere to get away from it all, then totally, use my room."

"Thanks. I swear I won't abuse the privilege."

"And I swear to wear clothes."

They both laughed. Christian offered a friendly hand and they shook. Then they toasted with their remaining half glasses and started to clear the table.

NOAH BEGAN spending time in Christian's guest room, mostly in the mornings or during little breaks throughout the day, and Christian began finding reasons to be in his room also.

Finding excuses is more like it, he admitted to himself with an internal smile. He liked being around Noah as the days dragged on, and he liked even more that Noah liked being around him.

One day he walked into his own bedroom, wearing a long-sleeved denim shirt and work gloves because he was there to collect junk pieces of wood that the plumbers wanted to use as a ramp or something, and Noah was there sitting on the bed with his laptop. Christian's eyes went wide before he checked himself: Noah wasn't wearing a shirt.

The heat finally got to him, Christian thought with a chuckle, and he was about to say something to that effect when it hit him that he should do no such thing. Noah looked up at him, smiled, said nothing, and went back to his computer, where he was no doubt writing about wine, reading about wine, or databasing wine. The moment was so casual that Christian realized making a joke would ruin it. It had taken so long to get Noah to come out of his shell (no pun intended) that Christian didn't want him to think he was making fun.

And what was under Noah's "shell" did not disappoint. From his surreptitious glances, Christian could tell that Noah's physique wasn't as toned, his musculature not as defined as his own. That said he was certainly not out of shape. The skin on his chest was as pale as the skin on his face, and even if he hadn't already said so, Christian could've guessed at his background as a swimmer. The hairless abs and pecs were built of tight, wiry muscle, and while he wouldn't be competing in any bodybuilding competitions, he looked like he could've carried his own weight if Christian had ever asked him to help out around the villa.

Most tempting of all to Christian's eye, each pectoral was topped with a small, almost delicate nipple, no bigger than dimes but dark brown in contrast to the pale white skin that surrounded them. For one beautiful moment, Christian entertained the thought of sucking on those nipples until Noah cried out in pleasure from underneath him.

"Did... did you need me for something?" Noah asked.

Christian realized he was staring and shook his head, both to clear his attention and to answer the question. "Nah, just gotta grab some of the beat-up old wood. Hope the bed's comfy, slacker."

Noah laughed, and Christian went on about the business of heaving wood back to the team, followed by the business of reminding

61

the team that they'd already had their coffee and cigarette break for the morning.

The more he thought about that moment, the more it built up inside of him. Was Noah flirting with him after all? Had he picked up on Christian's cues, despite them probably being too subtle? Was there a chance for Christian, far more hesitant and cautious than the stereotype of a Miami jock might make one think, to see even more of Noah?

It was on a Friday that all hell finally broke loose. After a long day of overseeing contractors, assisting in the installation of new fixtures all over the villa, even a little light demolition work when it became clear that the plans for the backyard patio were going to have to be completely redone, Christian saw the workmen off and went to the kitchen to collapse. Noah was there, cooking as per their unspoken agreement regarding dinner, his back to Christian as he came in. Christian did exactly as he intended: he collapsed, his entire frame landing on a rustic wooden chair hard enough that he feared it might come crashing down under him. He rubbed his sweaty brow with the bottom of his tank top.

"Oh man, you would not believe the day I had. Well actually yeah, you probably heard most of it. What's for dinner?"

Noah turned around to face him with an expression Christian had never seen before. That nigh-cherubic face, with its blond locks and blue eyes behind the black-rimmed glasses, looked ugly... downright menacing. He experienced the previously unknown sensation of having Noah glare at him.

"Uh... huh?" was the most articulate Christian could be when caught off guard.

Noah continued to glare, absently turning whatever was sizzling in the pan in front of him.

"Was it something I said?"

Noah gestured with one finger, beckoning him. "C'mere a minute," he said and walked out of the room.

Tired as he was from the grueling day, Christian got up and followed. If something had his new friend upset, he wanted to know about it. They arrived at the door to Noah's room, and Noah pushed it open without stepping in.

"Oh... oh my God," Christian said as he surveyed the damage. "I'm so sorry. I had no idea anyone was even in here today."

The place was chaos. A large canvas drop cloth had been laid on the floor, large enough to cover Noah's bed as well. It was filthy with dirt and grime and Christian could see why: huge sections of the ceiling had been removed. Bare wiring was exposed where the electrician had clearly been working. Apart from the bed, which had been too big to move more than a few feet, everything in the room had been shifted into a far corner in order to get out of the contractors' way. Christian wasn't sure how long it had been since they'd been working there, but dust still hung heavy in the air.

The bathroom, its new toilet and polished new fixtures, sat pristine and almost mocking them.

"I am so sorry, man," Christian repeated, his attention drawn mostly to the bare wires. "It is definitely not safe to sleep in here. But hey, at least the bathroom works, right?"

He looked at Noah to gauge his reaction to the joke and found it was not the reaction he'd hoped for.

"This is a goddamned nightmare!" Noah cried out, startling Christian not only with the explosion of volume but also with the tears in his eyes. "This is fucking insane! I swear, the only thing I asked for was a place to sleep for the night and I don't even have that anymore!"

"Woah," Christian said. "Are you saying this is my fault?"

"Aren't you in charge of them?"

Christian decided that Noah had him there. "Okay, yes, but like I said, I didn't know anyone was going to be in here today. They're supposed to ask my approval any time they want to go tearing up the place, but a couple of the electricians can be kind of overzealous."

"That still doesn't—"

"And it's still my fault," Christian said, refusing to be interrupted. "The work is my responsibility. I'm sorry. It won't happen again."

Noah seemed to be calming down. Christian supposed that there was more going on than the unexpected demolition, the stress of being relegated to just the basement and someone else's bedroom probably starting to take its toll.

Maybe even a bit of homesickness, he guessed.

"Thanks," Noah said. "I appreciate it. But where am I going to sleep tonight?"

"You'll sleep in my room," Christian told him without missing a beat. "It's my fault. I'll fix it. My bed's got clean sheets, and I'll sleep on the floor."

Noah looked at him skeptically. "It's a king-size bed. You're not sleeping on the floor. If we were, like, going to be on top of each other, then maybe, but with that much space, we can figure it out."

Christian's heart gave a little jump at the thought of sharing a bed with Noah, even in the most platonic way, and he tried not to smile.

"Okay then, sounds good."

They returned to the kitchen just in time to save dinner and had a quiet meal. Christian felt like Noah had forgiven him, but he didn't want to push his luck, and Noah didn't seem to have much to say. Christian made a token effort, asking what was up in the wine cellar that day, and Noah responded. He asked what had made Christian's day so difficult, and Christian regaled him with tales of the brutality, but wrapped it up when he sensed that Noah's mind was elsewhere.

Truth be told, his own mind was elsewhere too.

They parted ways at Noah's door, Noah intent on picking through the debris to find something he could wear to sleep in and Christian off to get in and out of his bathroom before Noah needed it. Just as Christian was crawling under the sheets, there came the knock he'd expected at the door.

"Knock, knock," Noah said, pushing the door open.

"Not by the hair of my chinny-chin-chin," Christian replied, and Noah laughed at last.

He was wearing the same clothes he'd been in when the two of them had their shower incident. White-and-blue striped boxers and a blue T-shirt, the fly on the boxers securely and obviously fastened this time. He had one hand over his eyes.

"Tell me you're decent," he said.

"Never," Christian replied. "But for you, yeah, I'll sleep with some clothes on tonight."

Noah took the hand away, still smiling, and Christian felt those eyes on his body. By "some clothes" Christian hadn't meant more than a pair of gray boxer briefs, but he was encouraged by the thought that Noah might like what he was seeing.

"I finished up in the bathroom in case you needed it," he said.

"No, I used mine," Noah replied. "Like you said, at least that works."

Christian reached behind him to fluff up his pillow while Noah walked around and got in on the far side of the bed. As expected, there was at least a foot or two of space between them. Christian, who liked to roll around a lot, resolved to be on his best behavior. When Noah was settled, he spoke up.

"You all good over there?"

"Yeah," Noah sighed. "I just want to forget all about this day."

"I hear that. Night, Noah."

"Good night, Christian."

Christian hit the switch at the bedside table that controlled the lights, and the room grew dim. Not quite fully dark, though: that big, bright, beautiful moon shone through the glass doors. The moon from his childhood visiting Granddad in the summer. The Italian moon that somehow looked different to him than any other moon in the world was shining on him tonight, giving the room a glow that he swore he'd never noticed before.

Beside him, across the bed but still somehow in bed with him, this handsome man who he had met through the most random of good fortune alone was out like a light. Noah soon began to snore. Not a deep, rumbling sound that might have been hard to sleep through, just a louder-than-usual breathing. Christian thought he sounded like a kitten snoring softly in the night.

It was that thought he took with him as he drifted off to sleep.

CHAPTER 10

THE MOMENT he awoke, not normally a morning person to begin with, Noah was confused. It took him a moment to get his bearings.

This isn't my room, he thought. That brought back memories of the previous afternoon, when he'd discovered his own bedroom in a state of monstrous disrepair, and the near-fight he'd almost had with Christian over it.

This isn't my bed, he thought, before the previous memory led right into the one where Christian had graciously agreed to share.

This isn't my... what is this?

His first thought was that he'd become tangled up in sheets or pillows while he slept, or that maybe he'd rolled against a wall somehow. And then he felt the breathing. There was a body pressed against him.

A hard, muscled body at that. He heard that low, regular breathing that said his bedmate was still asleep. He felt the warmth behind him and smelled that scent that was uniquely Christian, an odor he'd detected once or twice from simply living together but more often when in proximity. The first association his mind made with that mature, tantalizing musk was a sense of safety and care.

He looked down to find that tanned arm he knew so well wrapped around his midsection, thick muscles lightly evident under the skin as the arm squeezed him tighter. The downy dark hairs on the back of that arm were softer than Noah had realized, now that he saw them up close.

Ultimately he was forced to acknowledge another part of Christian seemed like it wanted attention too. Pressed against his lower back was the unmistakable sensation of Christian's dick, and

Noah reveled in it. What had seemed impressive enough now brought him new wonder and disbelief as he felt the whole length of the thing running along behind him. It was hard to guess without his eyes for assistance, but the dick had to be at least eight or more inches long and thick as well.

A grower and *a shower*, Noah thought, allowing himself a mischievous smile since Christian was still asleep anyway. The mere idea, accompanied by the feeling of that gorgeous piece of equipment pressed tightly against him, was enough to awaken something lustful and potent inside of him, something he'd been trying to avoid since the day he'd met the other man. His own member began to stir, expanding to its full rigidity below and out of sight, and the sensation overwhelmed him. It was tangled uncomfortably in the bedsheets and boxers below his waist, and he moved around, trying to dislodge himself.

The rubbing of his own cock against the fabric did nothing to ease that tension.

Neither did he relax when he realized he was basically grinding against Christian's crotch in order to disentangle. No sooner had he thought it than he felt a low, growling moan coming from the man who held him.

He stopped moving. Was Christian awake? Was this about to get awkward?

For the first time since his arrival, possibly the first time in his life, Noah decided to listen to that voice inside, the lustful one that cried out for attention and release. He continued to tug at the sheets, eventually working himself free, attempting to stay oblivious of Christian's state of awareness for as long as possible.

It was only when he stopped moving that he felt Christian grinding right back. That thick, warm, beautiful shaft was slowly sliding up and down the length of Noah's ass crack, the fabric of both men's undergarments keeping any skin-to-skin contact from happening but the friction between them undeniably erotic and powerful. Slow, grinding strides from the cleft of Noah's bottom to the dimples at his tailbone, soon gave way to rougher, brazen thrusts.

"Christian," Noah mewled, almost without realizing he'd done so, at the sheer pleasure of it.

The thrusting stopped. Noah heard Christian's deep, husky voice whispering into his ear. His words were at once both insistent and gentle, patient but intoxicating.

"Tell me to stop and I'll stop," he said, and Noah had no doubt of his promise.

Noah shut his eyes and moved his back closer to Christian's nearly naked body. He wrapped an arm around the other man, pressing at his back to draw him even closer.

"Don't stop," Noah whispered.

Christian continued his sensual frottage, rubbing that powerful dick up and down, up and down, pressing hard enough from time to time that he was eventually pressing the shaft right against Noah's hole. It felt so good that Noah was afraid his mind might actually melt, both the startling closeness of the other man and the titillating reminder that if he wanted it, that cock could go deeper still. All he had to do was ask. Noah wondered if this was what heaven was like.

He soon learned what heaven really was when he felt the arm around him slide down to his abdomen, then to his pubic bone, then the feeling of Christian's hand as it slipped inside his boxers and wrapped around his own flesh. The rough, calloused fingers of the handyman withdrew suddenly, Noah heard a familiar organic sound, and when they returned, they were slick and ready to stroke.

The mewling within Noah changed into a growl. As Christian slid his hand up and down, Noah felt hungry, horny, desperate for release.

Their movements synched up perfectly, to an extent Noah had never experienced before. With each thrust of his sweaty cock into Christian's hand, the big man behind him pulled back, and with each grind of his ass against Christian's manhood, he felt it swell with excitement and urgency. It was unlike any sex Noah had ever had, made all the hotter for its spontaneity and its primal drive.

Christian rutted against him like a beast, and Noah let him, savoring the thrill of that powerful organ tickling at his hole until, grunting, Christian announced, "I'm coming."

The statement only drove Noah to harder, wilder thrusts, his eagerness to please Christian matched only by the intense joy he too was receiving from the other man's hand. It wasn't long before he felt his partner's orgasm, the thrusting changing to throbbing while Christian sighed, loud and long, as if to keep himself from crying out.

Noah stopped his grinding against Christian's cock but was lost in the throes of divine rapture as the other man tightened his grip, ever so gently, and sped up his motion. The hand, warm and tight yet slick around Noah's penis, moved back and forth, generating friction. In his untamed lust, when strange thoughts come upon one suddenly, Noah thought that it was surely an indisputable sign of true love when a partner's orgasm wasn't enough, when they cared enough to bring you to your own completion.

And Christian cared. Alternating speeds, wrapping his hand over, under, and around, he groped at Noah's intimate flesh using delicate maneuvers that Noah could imagine how he'd learned. At last, his muscles weary from tension and his throat dry from groaning with pleasure, Noah exploded violently, crying out as he did so, waves of passion shuddering from the tips of his toes to the crown of his head.

As they lay there, the two lovers, for that was what they had become, entangled in sheets and fluids, Noah felt for one perfect moment that he had experienced something truly magical. He pulled Christian's arm around his waist, not wanting the moment to end.

When it did, though, a wave of long-held self-doubts came with it, washing over Noah and leaving him a nervous wreck.

What the fuck was that? he asked himself. *It was so, so good but…. Oh my god, did I just make the biggest mistake of my life?*

Worries ran through his head, each more terrible than the last. Christian had said yes, had even asked him to consent, but what if it was just in the heat of the moment? What if Christian never looked at him the same way again? It killed him to imagine Christian, whose friendship he'd come to treasure in a few short weeks, never wanting to make eye contact with him again lest he be reminded of what had happened. Worse, what if Christian lost respect for him? Hated him for taking advantage of the handyman's morning wood?

Worst of all, in the darkest corners of Noah's mind, he asked himself, *What if I was no good at it?* Rather, what if Christian held it against him that he hadn't allowed himself to be taken, really and truly taken, right there in the bed? The idea of it was enticing, he had to admit, but that made it all the more awful to imagine Christian thinking he was some kind of weirdo or prude. When he thought about the two of them grinding against each other like college kids fumbling in the dark, as if they were anxious not to wake up someone else... or even worse, the notion that Christian might think him so inexperienced, or kinky, or scared... it unnerved him.

Gently, he pulled away and Christian let him go. In the early morning light, he collected himself, stepped out through the bedroom door, and went back to his own room to shower and clean up.

BEFORE HE knew what was happening, Christian heard his bedroom door click shut. Noah was gone. *What went wrong?*

He reviewed the frolicking in his memory and found it sweet, adorable almost, a touching and intimate way for two lovers to begin to get to know each other without pressure or regret... but it was obvious Noah didn't feel that way.

Sullen, Christian got out of bed, pulled off the sheets, and set them aside to wash, then threw his own damp boxer briefs into the pile along with them. The morning light was taking on an unfortunately gray cast. There was a storm on the horizon, he had no doubt.

It took a moment to get the shower as hot as he liked it, but when he finally did get the chance to scrub away the sweat, his mind was only on Noah. The shocking moment in that very bathroom when they'd first shared an intimacy, Noah seemingly unable to keep himself from checking out Christian's body and his dick. The view he'd had of Noah's sexy little nipples, and then what had happened just moments ago....

Christian felt that insatiable organ between his legs beginning to rise once more and willed it into submission. If what they'd done had caused Noah to run from him, without even a word, then it was clear it could never happen again. And he'd better get used to the idea.

A half hour later, fully clothed, he walked past Noah's door, which was shut. He considered knocking, tumbling over words in his head as he tried to think of something that wouldn't make things even more awkward but unable to do so.

Fancy degree in communications and I never know what to say around him, Christian thought, chiding himself as he walked away and down the hall to the kitchen. *Should've at least made sure he closed his pool doors before the storm gets here.*

In the mood for a light breakfast only and remembering how Noah had mentioned once that he liked fruit, Christian cut up a bunch of different fresh fruits into a bowl... and then a second bowl. Maybe what he couldn't say with words he could say with a gesture they had both come to understand. After gobbling down his own meal, he set the other bowl at Noah's place on the table, along with a note that just had one extra-big smiley face.

Looking out onto the pool area, he saw that Noah's pool access doors were shut also. *Another excuse to talk to him, gone.*

As soon as the workmen arrived he harangued them, yelling harder than he had in a long time, feeling his face get red. He demanded to know which one had rendered his roommate's room unlivable and insisted that fixing it should be the first priority of the day. The men shrugged and got to work. It was Christian's first sign that Noah was up and about, the fact that when they came to his room the door was ajar and he was nowhere to be seen. His laptop was gone also, suggesting he was likely hard at work down in the wine cellar. It gave him hope. He'd been afraid Noah might be the type to sulk or something. At least if he was sulking, it wasn't in his room.

When he stopped for lunch, he saw that the fruit had been eaten, the bowl washed and left in the dish dryer. The note with the smiley face was gone. He took it as another hopeful sign.

His hopes for Noah's room were less likely to bear fruit. The repairs happened in near-record time, but he'd had a sinking feeling from the start that there was no way they'd be done by nighttime. The ceiling was patched up, but the smell of having done so was abhorrent. With the drop cloths removed, Christian made them clean up all the dirt they had left behind, though they complained the whole time that it was a job for cleaners, not for licensed workers. They all wanted to leave, to get to their homes before the storm hit. Christian could hardly blame them. Some of them had to take dirt roads for at least part of the trip, and he didn't want them to risk washing out on his behalf.

They packed it up for the day just as the first heavy drops were beginning to fall, and Christian walked down to the end of the drive in order to wave them off, thank them, and wish them the best. It was well before sundown, but the skies were so dark that it might just as well have been night already. For his troubles he got drenched with thick drops of water on his way back up to the house, and his boots tramped through far more mud than he had ever wanted to see on the tiled floors of the villa, his beautiful charge. It was a crummy end to a crummy day.

Worst of all, Noah's room, while mostly finished, reeked of chemicals that would have to air out overnight.

Devastated, Christian hung his head hung low as he stopped to strip off his boots just inside the entryway. On taking a whiff of himself, he also unbuttoned his denim shirt to let it air out. Noah could handle the sight of his chest, he was sure.

As he was undoing the laces of the boots, he smelled olive oil and something acidic, tomatoes maybe. Had Noah forgiven him? Would he turn the corner into that kitchen to find a welcome meal, dinner for two so they could put it all behind them? Or, he feared, dinner only for one because Noah would never look at him again?

The safest thing to do seemed to be check beforehand. "Is that dinner?" he called tentatively into the kitchen from the foyer.

"You bet," came Noah's voice floating back.

"Dinner... for two?" he asked, and was at once disappointed with how pathetic and needy his voice sounded. As if how Noah felt about him really mattered... which, he supposed, it did.

"Come in and see," came the reply, with just a hint of playfulness about it, and Christian's heart leapt. He pulled off the shoes, left the shirt open, and stepped through the kitchen doorway.

What he saw dispelled his fears and brought a smile to his face like he hadn't felt in a long, long time.

Noah was there, at the stove, stirring something in a heavy iron pan. He turned his head over one shoulder and smiled at Christian, his seductive blue eyes penetrating from the black-rimmed glasses he wore.

He also wore a red cooking apron that hung from his neck down to his knees. And nothing else.

Christian allowed himself a moment to really drink in the sight of Noah's perfect, gorgeous ass. It was round and full, a product of good genes, though years of a swimming regimen couldn't possibly have hurt. The lights were on in the kitchen to combat the growing darkness outside, and in their soft glow, Christian thought he could almost count the thousand little blond hairs on Noah's ass. The way Noah's shoulder blades curved above the knobs of his spine, of which Christian could make out one or two, and then tracing that spine down to the dimples above that beautiful behind.... Christian saw Noah's shoulders moving, and he realized that other man was arching his back so he could present a better view. Never in his life had Christian seen anything more inviting.

Except, perhaps, for Noah's smile.

"Dinner will be ready in a minute," he said, raising his eyebrows in an innocent wrinkle. "I hope you like what I have planned for dessert."

"You... I mean, wow," Christian said, and Noah blushed. "It's a compliment," he clarified before Noah could take it the wrong way. "You are glorious."

"Thank you."

"I have to ask, though," Christian began, afraid he might ruin the moment but even more afraid of not making absolutely certain, "You seemed... I don't know, unhappy after this morning. I thought I came on too strong or scared you off. I thought maybe I'd hurt your feelings. What changed your mind?"

"You did, silly." Noah turned to face him, taking a step to one side in order to lean his bare backside on the kitchen counter rather than the hot stove. Christian was able to see the meal at last, vegetables steaming in the pan and a bottle of white wine that sat nearby. The label said "Vernaccia di San Gimignano," and Christian watched as Noah took a long pull from one of the two glasses beside it. He never took his eyes off Christian as he drank.

"I had all day to think about this morning," Noah said, "and the thought I came up with was, well, y'know. Life is too short."

Christian grinned.

"You're into me, I'm into you," Noah went on, setting the glass down. He reached over to the stove and turned the burner off. "Seems to me there's an obvious solution to that. As for where it goes, well...."

"Yeah?"

"If it's just 'that wonderful summer in Tuscany,' then that's just fine with me."

Christian felt a powerful urge to cross the kitchen and take Noah in his arms, and at last he gave in to that desire. He closed the distance between them in two strides and pressed his lips to Noah's, an action Noah reciprocated wholeheartedly. He wrapped his arms around the other man, feeling the bare skin of Noah's back in contrast to the crisp fabric of the apron that covered his front. The duality was tantalizing to Christian: starched fabric pressed against his nipples, which were exposed by his unbuttoned shirt and smooth and sensitive skin in both his hands. The thought of undoing that apron like he was unwrapping a package made his mouth water.

Noah's mouth moved in perfect time to his own, lips opening and closing to meet Christian's, his tongue alternately exploring the inside of Christian's mouth and receding to allow him the same indulgence. The warmth and closeness was like a drug to Christian, the barest scent of an aftershave that he'd smelled on Noah before now delivering waves of euphoria from up close. When his lips reached too far out and he encountered stubble, growing on a man who hadn't bothered shaving in a day or two, he became all the more eager to explore the rest of Noah's body.

They kissed for a few moments, as if the sweet kisses were an appetizer for things to come. For his part, Christian was simply enjoying the first simple pleasures before moving on to something more.

When Noah was ready for that something more, he made it known unambiguously. There could be no doubts left by swelling in his groin from underneath the apron, the pressure from his cock that mounted by the second as it pushed against Christian's own. Christian pulled his mouth away from Noah's and looked down into those amazing blue eyes and he knew.

Tenderly Christian ran his hands down the length of Noah's body, one on either side, as he lowered them to Noah's hips. He felt all along Noah's soft skin outside the boundaries of the cooking apron and enjoyed the tease of what he hoped was to come. In one smooth motion, he hoisted Noah up and seated that lovely bare bottom on the kitchen counter. Then, a mock lascivious smile on his lips, he lifted the lower portion of the apron, rested it on the back of his head, and got to work.

The lusty smile got a laugh from his lover, as he'd hoped it would, but the work of his mouth and tongue turned the laughter to sighs and then moans. Noah's cock, which only his hand had known before, was now prey to both his eyes and his lips. It was magnificent, circumcised, full and glistening in the amber glow that passed from the kitchen lights through the red apron, a pale, veiny shaft that turned to pink just before it ended in a large reddish mushroom crown.

Christian wrapped both lips tightly around the organ and thrust down, deep down until he found the hilt, until he could feel the tip resting against the far back of his throat.

He sucked greedily and breathed in deep as his nose was buried in Noah's pubic hair. It was soft, not wiry like some he'd met before, and looked red itself under the lighting conditions, but the smell rather than the feel was what drove him wild. It was so masculine, lightly scented of soap but also tinged with sweat, and so uniquely Noah that the closeness of it alone was pushing him over the edge.

Christian wrapped his right hand around the base of the shaft as he slowly moved up and down its length, but his left he curled around Noah's balls and began to tug, very gently. From the moans that issued from Noah's lips, growing in both volume and intensity, he took the hint that he was doing something right. He continued to pull, his touch light as he cradled them like precious jewels, his hand moving in time with his mouth.

So great was his desire for Noah, and even greater his desire for Noah's pleasure, that before he even noticed it, he was doing something he'd never done before. A guy back in Miami had once ended each full slide along the shaft with a lick of the tongue, around the ridge of the head and right over the slit, and it had driven Christian to ecstasy. He tried it on Noah, and when he felt the other's whole body shudder under his ministrations, he smiled to himself and gleefully did it again.

He felt the lower part of the apron, still draped over the back of his head while he gorged himself on cock, come loose: Noah had undone the strings. He felt as it was pulled to one side, his furtive action exposed to the open air, and to his immense pleasure he felt Noah's hands wrap around the back of his head where the apron had just been. As he bobbed up and down on Noah's cock, he felt his lover's fingers tangle into his hair and then felt them grip the hair ever so slightly. Noah pulled, just a little bit, and Christian was over the moon.

He felt a tap at the back of his head and looked up from his labors to meet Noah's gaze. The other man was flushed, his whole pale body turning red, and he wasn't breathing so much as panting. The moaning had given way to quick, shallow breaths, and sweat was running down his forehead like the rivulets of water on the panes of glass at the kitchen window. A flash of lightning struck as Noah smiled.

"Not yet," he finally said. "Not yet. I want you. I… want you."

His mind on other things (or, rather, one thing in particular), it took Christian a moment to figure out what Noah meant. When he did he pulled his mouth off of Noah's organ, long, wet and slow-moving as he did so, and grinned.

"Are you sure?"

Noah nodded vigorously, and Christian grinned even wider. Off in the distance, answering the lightning, a burst of thunder rolled.

Christian stood up, and Noah pulled the open apron up and over his head and flung it aside. Finally his whole naked body was on display for Christian's eager eyes and hands. He reached under Christian's open denim shirt and drew his hands over Christian's bare chest, teasingly encircling the right nipple as he did so, to Christian's delight. Finally he pulled the shirt off entirely and reached down to the denim shorts.

"I've been waiting almost a month to get these things off you," he said as he undid the first button.

"Really?"

Noah cocked an eyebrow at him. "You didn't see it? I thought I was so obvious, that you'd think I was a creep or something."

Christian laughed. "That's what I thought you would think about me!"

They laughed together as Noah undid the other buttons of Christian's fly. He thought fleetingly of helping, but Noah seemed to be having so much fun working the denim around the buttons.

I got to unwrap my present, he considered. *Let him have the same good time if he wants it that bad.*

Noah did want it bad. When he finally had the denim cutoffs undone, spattered as they were with huge drops of water from his time outside, Noah tried to slide them down Christian's thighs... to no avail.

Christian looked down. The tight shorts were caught on his erection, the hardest he could ever recall being, the outline of which pointed up to the sky from underneath the material of his light gray boxer briefs. A dark spot at the top demonstrated Christian's first, unplanned offerings to their rapture, a precursor and promise of things yet to come.

"Someone's happy to see me," Noah commented with a light giggle.

"Heh. I got it," Christian said, reaching down.

"No, let me," Noah replied, so Christian stood, arms at his sides, while the other tugged at the shorts. First one side, then the other. There was no way around Christian's manhood.

"Nothing for it," Noah finally said, and with one hand he grasped Christian's cock, sending ripples of pleasure throughout the other man's entire body.

Christian gasped. Noah smiled.

With a touch as light as if he were working a marionette, Noah tugged Christian's cock this way and that in order to get it out of the way of the denim. As the shorts began to come off, Christian was practically crazed from the teasing feeling of that soft hand through cotton on his erection. He ached for release and growled in hopes it might hurry Noah forward.

As if in response, the lightning flashed again.

The cutoff shorts made it over his groin and down, where Noah had to tug a little more to get them over Christian's thighs, and they hit the ground with a slap. Christian figured they must've been wetter than he supposed.

"Moment of truth...," Noah said, and then lifted the waistband of the underwear up and over Christian's cock. When he saw the whole thing, not rested and flaccid from a recent shower but engorged with desire and ready for action, his eyes got wide, a thing that caused Christian no small amount of joy.

"It's so beautiful," Noah whispered. "I thought when I saw it that it couldn't get any bigger but…."

"Oh, it gets pretty big," Christian admitted.

Noah wrapped one hand around it and then the other. The lower hand was halfway down Christian's balls, but from above it looked as if Noah had gotten both hands on the shaft. Christian couldn't resist a little manly pride that his dick might be a two-hander.

Noah played with one finger around the foreskin. The far-off thunder rumbled again.

"See, now I get what's going on here," Christian said. "I thought foreplay was over, but somebody just likes to tease a little, doesn't he?" Noah's laugh in response was on the border of being a giggle. "Well, two can play that game."

Christian put his left hand around Noah's back and his right on Noah's balls… and then below Noah's balls. He began delicately stroking, poking at that warm, inviting place, that hole he'd known for the invitation it was from the first time he'd laid eyes on that beautiful ass. With his first finger, he increased pressure on Noah's most sensitive spot.

Noah's eyes practically rolled back in his head, and he moaned, his two hands gripping even harder on Christian's shaft. Christian went deeper.

He reached for a nearby bottle of olive oil, and soon both hands were slick as he went about his work, holding Noah in place while he drew that finger in and out, soon followed by a second finger, as eager as his partner to bury his cock inside that ass all the way up to the balls but wanting to make sure that opening was ready to receive his proud, thick member.

"Okay, I'm sorry!" Noah said in a voice that was half laughter and half ecstatic scream. "I'm ready. I'm so ready! Fuck me, Christian! Fuck me hard!"

Christian needed no more encouragement. He flipped Noah's legs up above his shoulders, exposing that welcoming hole that he had felt but not yet seen, and Noah leaned back on the kitchen counter on his elbows, then his back. Christian's foreskin slid back to display the shining purple head, and Noah guided the piece down into the depths of his cleft and then inside.

Noah reacted to the pressure at his asshole by closing his eyes and biting his lower lip, but when Christian ceased pushing forward he was suddenly nodding, indicating that the reaction was a pleasurable one, pulling at Christian's arms, which still held him by the hips, so that his lover would know he was ready for more. Slowly at first, Christian moved deeper and deeper within him, Noah all the while making that little mewling sound that Christian remembered from the morning, urging him to push deeper still. Noah was so warm, the wet hole tight around his cock, that Christian didn't even notice that he was all the way in until he felt Noah's balls against his abdomen. Taking the genitals and lifting them carefully out of the way, Christian began to pull out and then to press in once more.

Soon he was slapping his testicles against Noah's behind, and the small, kittenish cries the other man was issuing from his place on the kitchen counter had turned into excited screams that wavered between pleasure and some kind of deep, animal growl. Christian became lost in the moment, sliding up and down, hammering again and again, conscious only of the enveloping warmth around his cock and of Noah's cries, which escaped his lips in time with the thrusts. Christian imagined hitting Noah's prostate again and again, slamming that button with his cock like a fairgoer ringing a bell with a sledgehammer. The lightning crashed, and the thunder roared outside.

"I'm gonna... I'm gonna..." were the only words of warning that Noah was able to get out before the liquid proof of his orgasm exploded from his still tumescent cock. Christian took it in one hand to help milk it to completion, but he soon saw he needn't have bothered: Noah's orgasm was a powerful one. It splashed on his pubic hair, his chest, his right nipple. Christian even noticed with humor that some got on the window behind them that looked out onto the pool.

"Ugghh," Noah said, and some other unintelligible animal sounds as Christian too reached his climax. He felt it in a way he never had before, the sensation of his orgasm building from deep within his balls up and out through the shaft still thrust fully inside Noah's smooth, round ass. Noah cried once more, a high-pitched thing that tried and failed to put a word to the indescribable feeling of Christian filling him up inside with the warm fluid evidence of their lovemaking, contrasted by the potent growl that issued from Christian's throat.

The lightning flashed, and almost immediately afterward, the thunder roared.

CHAPTER 11

IN THE morning the workmen were forced to let themselves in. It was no trouble, the villa's door wasn't locked, just unusual because Christian was usually there to greet them by the time they arrived. The lead man checked his watch and pointed out to the others that they were earlier than usual so perhaps their young boss was still having breakfast.

They set to work. Some headed out to the back patio to inspect any potential damage from the storm, others to the pool, which should need only a few basic touches before the specialists were called in, still others to the second guest bedroom that the boss had indicated was a priority. The electrician, taking advantage of the stillness in the house, went to inspect the wiring in the basement in hopes of completing his survey and plans there before the other of the two gentlemen appeared.

The lead man, finding no evidence of either man in the kitchen, went to the guest room at the end of the hall, which he knew the young boss had taken for personal use. He called lightly to the signore but received no response. He went to rap a knuckle on the door, and it swung open under his hand.

Lying in the bed, facing away from him, was the young boss. He was naked, a proud specimen of Italian manhood, and the lead man realized that he was still asleep. What's more, he saw that the young boss had his arm wrapped around someone. Craning his neck to see, he made out the form of the other gentleman, also naked, pale, with his legs crossed as if for modesty. It was like something out of a painting, the two asleep side by side with Noah the little spoon.

Smiling to himself, the lead workman shut the door behind him as he left. The other men, noticing his smile, asked him what had provoked such a reaction.

"*L'amore*" was all he would say.

Chapter 12

"We should get up."

"You get up."

"Smart ass."

"Horndog."

Noah knew Christian would take that one to heart and he did, delivering a sharp but playful slap on Noah's bare behind. Noah squealed.

After the evening's events, they had fallen into Christian's bed together and awoke right around the same time yet again, or perhaps Christian had been up first. Noah wasn't certain. All he knew for sure was that he awoke naked, a gorgeous man folding his arms around him from behind who was also naked, and the refreshing Tuscan sunshine spilling into the room like water from a carafe. One of the french doors was ajar, leading out into the garden, and he watched a green woodpecker flit from one small tree to the next. A white curtain over the glass panes of the door fluttered in the breeze.

Possessed by an urge to see his lover with his own eyes, Noah rolled around until they were once more face-to-face. Christian lay on the pillow beside him, smiling and gazing at him groggily as he blinked the evening's sleep out of his eyes. Out of pure impishness Noah stole a glance below, only to discover that Christian's lower extremity was also, once again, ready to report for duty.

Noah made no move to take hold of it, nor to initiate anything, and neither did Christian. They took full advantage of the opportunity to just stare into each other's eyes. It was Christian who broke the stare.

"I hate to say it," he said, looking up and down Noah's body. "In fact I really, really hate to say it, but we should probably get up. It's well into the morning. I'm sure the guys are already here doing stuff. I want to supervise but even more I don't want them to think I'm the kind of guy who just lays around in bed while others do the heavy lifting."

"Absolutely," Noah agreed. "Gotta maintain the Caravelli name."

"Absolutely," Christian echoed. "Shower?"

"Go ahead, I don't mind," Noah said. "The workers won't care how long it takes me to go down into the wine cellar."

Christian stood up, and Noah appreciated the broad, curved lines of him until he stopped and turned around. Noah gave him a questioning eyebrow.

"My shower's bigger than yours, you know," he said. "Big enough for two."

Noah grinned.

They showered together, kissed some more, and then Christian dressed and went to join the workers. When he had signaled that they were completely out of Noah's room and off to work on other parts of the villa, Noah wrapped a towel around his waist and went to his own room to dress.

This he did with great difficulty. His mind kept wandering back to the night before, that fabulous night of amazing sexual adventure. He blushed all over again to think of himself taken in glorious fashion right there on a kitchen countertop. Never in his life had he been so brazen! It occurred to him that such a crazy escapade might be normal for Christian, who he was sure had to be more sexually experienced than he was, but he pushed that thought right out of his mind before it could take root.

Down that path lies doubt, he told himself, *doubt and insecurity. He seemed happy, I was happy, he was happy the next morning, and god knows so am I. He was even happy yesterday morning when all he fucked was the crack of my still-clothed ass!*

Consciously, intently, Noah allowed himself to just be happy. It was one of the best decisions he ever made.

His standard outfit of plaid short-sleeved button-down and khaki shorts in place, his glasses freshly cleaned and perched on his nose, he double-checked himself in the mirror. And smiled.

Grabbing his laptop, Noah headed down to the wine cellar to begin for the day. He'd left off in a mixed section, reds and whites of all different vintages across a span of different years just spread out all over the rack. The day before it had been so frustrating he'd been nearly pulling his hair out. What the hell was the point of a wine cellar if it had no organization? If you couldn't find anything when you wanted to find it? He briefly considered coming up with some signs to hang and clearly define each part of the cellar and what type of wine it was for. The image came to his mind of signs hanging over each rack, stylized little bundles of grapes at the end of each printed illustration, and he had to laugh at how he pictured the Cunninghams reacting. It would be like having a grocery store liquor department in your basement.

I'd get fired for sure, he thought, and went back to typing in his growing database.

It wasn't until around lunchtime that he realized he'd missed breakfast, his and Christian's attention having been elsewhere at the time. His stomach rumbled, and he knew there'd be plenty in the pantry that would satisfy him for a lunchtime snack, but his heart sank just a touch at the thought that it would be his first day without a little note from his roommate.

More than a roommate, he reminded himself for the pure glee of doing so.

After plugging his laptop in to charge, he went upstairs to the kitchen. All was quiet in the house, an unusual relief from the banging and hammering he'd become accustomed to. The workers had to be in a different part somewhere. Idly, not wanting to admit to himself that it mattered, he checked the kitchen table for a late breakfast he might've missed, a gift from Christian that would take on a new significance this time.

"No, there's no breakfast," came the voice at the patio doors, and Noah grinned before turning. There was Christian, leaning inward and holding the doorframe above him with both arms.

"Oh well," Noah said with a mock sigh. "Just as well I guess. I wouldn't want to get fat."

"Check the fridge," Christian said.

Noah opened the door and found a plate sitting at eye level. It held a turkey sandwich, the meat resting underneath lettuce and tomato fresh from some old grandmother's garden and between two slices of crusty wheat bread that had probably been baked less than a day before.

Next to the sandwich was a pickle and a bottle of diet soda. Noah laughed as he pulled out the ensemble.

"You have no idea how hard it was assembling a lunch worthy of a New York deli in the middle of Tuscany," Christian said.

Topping it all, resting on the bread where Noah hadn't seen it before, was a little white piece of paper with a note on it. It read "Sorry about breakfast" with a crude heart drawn under the lettering.

Noah kissed his lover, the man who'd brought him… if not New York, at least an interpretation of New York delivered by a Miami boy half raised in Italy.

WITH THE passionate floodgates open, the two drifted dreamily into a new sort of routine. Where before it had made Christian happy, this time it was sheer bliss.

They rose together in the mornings, early. He knew it annoyed Noah, but he insisted. Even after it became clear that the workmen knew exactly what was going on, Christian felt he'd be letting down both the Cunninghams and more importantly his grandfather if he didn't personally manage the renovation of the villa. Noah seemed to understand, saying more than once that his own professional reputation was at stake.

"I mean, I get that," Christian asked one morning as they showered together. "But it's not like you really want to be a sommelier all your life, is it?"

Noah didn't reply.

"Is it?"

Noah shrugged. "Maybe? I don't know. I do like wine, a lot. And art history is such a difficult field. Most who go into it wind up teaching, and I don't know if I want to teach."

"What else do they do?"

"Curate museums, write books," Noah replied, listing some ideas off the top of his head as he soaped a loofah over his chest.

Christian couldn't escape the notion that Noah sounded remarkably unenthused about the subject. He assumed that someone who competed to enter a graduate program in a given field would have already pictured the kind of career they'd like to come out of it with.

"Some just tour Italy endlessly," Noah added.

Christian smiled. "I could deal with that."

Noah returned the smile, and also the loofah. "Do my back."

When they were both ready to face the day, they had breakfast together, a new wrinkle in the routine but a welcome one. Christian made Noah coffee in an antique coffeepot his grandfather had loaned him, and Noah expanded the breakfast meal options with his array of knowledge around the kitchen. They tried to be done with breakfast before the workers arrived so the older Italian men wouldn't find them mooning over each other, but it didn't always work out. The first time they didn't make it they were just sitting down to eat when a bustle of workers came in through the door to the kitchen, on their way to the patio, and they both had to endure wolf whistles and catcalls. Christian had sworn at the men in good fun, and Noah had blushed but laughed also.

Christian's breakfast notes to Noah, which his lover seemed to appreciate, became a lunchtime gift instead. Dinner was unchanged, except perhaps with the addition of semiregular dessert in Christian's king-size bed. Unless one or the other was too tired from a truly exhausting day, both usually had the urge to strip off and jump in for the wild passion that tied them so closely together.

Although neither liked to discuss it, the day they would separate and it would all come to an end was ever-present in their minds.

Eventually, at the end of Noah's fourth week at the villa, marking about the halfway point of his stay in Italy, Silvio arrived to come and inspect the progress. Christian had been expecting him. Frankly he was surprised that his grandfather had left the project wholly in his hands for as long as he had. Standing in the doorway, Christian gave a big wave to the figure limping up from the end of the driveway. He had told his grandson that the leg was healing, but it was slow going.

The workmen, who knew Silvio from past associations, held the greatest respect for the old man. Christian was certain that despite his injury his grandfather wouldn't want any help walking, but he smiled to himself to see a couple of workmen following him a few paces behind in case the injured old builder should slip or fall.

He did not, and when he arrived at the door, he embraced his grandson. Christian was happy to see him, of course, the master about to throw a (hopefully) appreciative gaze over the work of the apprentice, but when they broke apart, he saw pain behind his granddad's smile.

"Are you all right?" he asked. "You didn't hurt yourself coming up the walk, did you?"

Silvio waved him off. "I'm all right. You worry too much. Let me see the villa."

"What is it, then?"

"Let me see the villa. Then we can talk."

Christian led him around, pointing out what was complete and what was not. As far as he was concerned the work was right on schedule, and his grandfather seemed to agree. He nodded with approval at the work Christian had done, almost entirely by himself, in the master bedroom. He toured the guest rooms, although when they reached Noah's room, he declined to enter.

"I can see fine from the doorway," he said.

"Oh, come on," Christian said with a little laugh. "Come look at the new glass in the doors to the pool. The glazer matched the remaining old panes perfectly!"

Silvio shook his head. "This boy, Noah, he is a guest in the home just like you and I. I will inspect the work, but I will not violate a man's privacy."

Christian shrugged and the tour continued.

He showed his grandfather the pool, which was almost complete, and the back patio, which had only just had the last stones laid that morning. The pool, he pointed out, was going to need some tile work, but he had yet to reach out to a restoration specialist.

"I didn't know how much the Cunninghams wanted to spend," he said. "They've sunk so much money into the place already, and we've done the retiling of the entryway. I didn't know if they'd want the whole mosaic restored."

"A good thought." Silvio nodded. "But the Americans have deep pockets, and Mrs. Cunningham is truly in love with this place. I tell you what: get a few quotes, take photographs, and send them to me by the email. I will write the Cunninghams and see what they prefer."

The tour ended in the kitchen, which had only ever needed minor repairs to begin with. Noah was nowhere in sight. Christian assumed he was busy working in the wine cellar, so he held out a chair at the kitchen table for the old man as he sat.

"Is this where you and he share the dinners I hear so much about?" Silvio asked with a twinkle in his eye.

Christian smiled.

"Aha!" his grandfather cried, clapping his hands. "My grandson, he blushes! I never thought I would see the day!"

"Granddad."

"Let an old man have his fun," Silvio said before sighing again.

"What's wrong?" Christian pressed him again. "You've had... I don't know, a sadness or something since you got here."

"All right," Silvio allowed. He placed the metal cane he'd been using to walk with against the kitchen table and leaned forward with both elbows. "It is about your parents."

"Mom and Dad? Is everything okay?"

His grandfather quieted him with both hands. "They are both fine. It is… it is the marriage that may not be."

Christian said nothing. He'd been afraid this news was coming.

"Your father wrote to me, just asking how you were and for all the news, and he told me that things are not going well. Your mother is a strong woman, as you know, demanding. He tells me there are questions that she has for him that he cannot answer. Or will not answer."

"Did he cheat on her?" The question escaped Christian's lips before he knew what he was saying, but in truth it had been on his mind ever since they had effectively sent him away for the summer.

Silvio sighed. "I… I do not know. He did not say he did, but—"

"But you heard something you didn't like to hear."

"Christian, this is what I come to say to you," the old man said, suddenly alive with energy and pointing sharply at his grandson with one finger. "The relationship between your parents, between those married, is not your relationship, and it is not your business. I know, I know, it's hard. I understand. But your parents are adults, as are you. Let them fix what is broken, or else leave the pieces and walk away. You don't get involved."

"How can I not be involved! I live there!"

"Christian—"

"What did he say that you didn't want to hear?" Christian had lowered his voice, but he wasn't asking anymore.

"He…." His grandfather sighed again and sat back once more. "He asked me to look into the annulment."

"Annulment?" Christian's eyes went wide. "How could they get an annulment after all this—"

"This is not important," Silvio returned. "As I say, you have your own life. It is time for you to live it without them."

As if a not-so-subtle reminder that there were people and things for him outside the umbrella of his parents' house, their friends, and the life he had back in Miami that might be crumbling from underneath him, Noah suddenly flung open the door from the wine cellar into the kitchen.

"It went down my shirt!" he was screaming hysterically. "It went down my goddamn shirt!"

Christian jumped to his side. "What? What happened?"

Noah was frantically patting at the red-and-white striped polo shirt he was wearing, blousing it open and shut at the bottom with his free hand.

"There's a freaking gigantic-ass enormous spider somewhere in my shirt!" he screamed.

Quick as a whip, without thinking, Christian grabbed Noah's shirt by the back of the neck and tugged upward. Noah held both arms up over his head. The shirt whirled right off of him, and Christian cast it to the ground between them. A big brown spider, almost as big as the palm of Christian's hand, crawled out of it.

"Tarantula!" cried Christian's grandfather. "Not to worry, friend. They are poisonous but couldn't kill anything bigger than a mouse."

Christian scooped up the spider with a nearby frying pan, carried it outside, and walked a good distance before depositing it in the bushes. When he came back, Silvio was explaining to a bewildered, still-shirtless Noah that this variety lived in caves around that part of Italy and that if he had been bitten, he would know it but that he needn't be afraid.

"It would feel like, you know, a bee sting," he was saying when Christian walked in the door. Noah looked at him wide-eyed.

Christian spun him around, inspected his back, then his chest, and then he smiled. "I think you're fine."

"I didn't feel any bites or anything," Noah admitted. "It just freaked me right out. Thanks."

"So!" Silvio said, beaming, "You must be the famous wine expert about which I've heard so much!"

Noah looked confused until Christian spoke up. "Noah, this is Silvio Caravelli, my grandfather."

"Oh!" Noah brightened, before deciding to cross his arms over his bare nipples. Christian managed to suppress his chuckle. "Nice to meet you!" he said, realizing that a handshake meant releasing at least one of his hands, which he did.

Christian's grandfather, however, laughed aloud. "It is nice to meet you too," he said, shaking the offered hand. "You can put your shirt back on if it makes you feel more comfortable."

Noah laughed, picking up the shirt and holding it instead. "It's great to finally make your acquaintance. Christian talks about you all the time."

"The boy is very kind."

"Will you stay for dinner?" Noah asked. "I have clams today. I was going to make a white sauce for some pasta."

"I'm sure Granddad has to be going," Christian said. Visions of embarrassing baby stories danced in his head.

"Nonsense!" Silvio cried. "I would be delighted! Do you need to start making your pasta now?"

"Making the pasta?" Noah responded, a quizzical look on his face.

"Oh, that'll do it," Christian muttered.

His grandfather's expression had turned to something between shock and abject horror. "You will be making the pasta, yes?"

Noah cast Christian a nervous glance.

"I never have…," he said.

"My boy!" Sr. Caravelli shouted, picking up his cane, "You will get an education today!"

CHAPTER 13

FOR THE first time since arriving at the villa, Noah did something he'd told himself he would never do: he took the afternoon off.

And what an education he got! He marveled at how the old man's hands, thick and strong from a life of building but wrinkled from age, were as nimble in the kitchen as they were mixing cement... maybe more so. He showed Noah how to make the well of flour on the countertop, to introduce egg yolks and salt, to stir and bring it all together into a dough for pasta. While the dough rested, the two of them scoured the cabinets.

"It must be here," Silvio grumbled.

"I hate to be a downer," Noah told him, "but I don't think it is. I've done a lot in this kitchen. If there was one here, I would've found it by now."

"Maybe so, maybe—aha!"

Noah turned to see the man holding up a metal apparatus, triumph in his eyes.

"Is that what that is? Sorry, I've never really seen one before. I figured that was a—"

"My boy, I tremble to think what you imagined this was for."

What Noah had assumed was some kind of mangle for thin cuts of meat turned out to be a roller for pasta dough. Christian's grandfather showed him how to set it up, how to turn the crank, and how to pass the dough through its wheels until he had long, thin sheets of pasta. Finally he showed how to give a final pass that would cut the pasta into linguini and toss the fresh pasta dough with semolina flour to keep it ready for use until he needed it.

It wasn't until they were halfway through the dough that Noah realized he'd never put his shirt back on. He laughed at himself when he did realize it, and quickly he ignored it also. Where before he might've been a little uptight about his body around strangers, he was definitely growing more casual. The notion that Christian's near-adoration of that body might be having an effect on him did occur to him.

Noah saw Christian a few times over the hour or two that he and Silvio cooked. The younger Caravelli was hard at work, leaving the other two some space to get to know each other, or so Noah hoped. He smiled at Christian whenever he walked through or past the kitchen, and Christian smiled back. If he was giving them space, Noah reasoned, then it was only one step removed from introducing Noah to his family.

Not a step at all, really, he thought.

On clam sauces the older man was less certain, his grounding in the kitchen and the preparation of respectable Italian dishes solid but his knowledge of seafood less so.

"I go to the sea," he admitted in a wavering voice, "for my health, or travel. I don't know the recipes, only what they taste like!"

Noah laughed. The Tuscan region of Italy was big, big enough that it wasn't unreasonable to think of the man having lived in the middle of the boot-shaped country all his life.

"Then if I may, sir," Noah said, "now *you* get the education."

Even as he said it, he felt bold, presumptuous, but Silvio laughed and clapped him on the back, and Noah took over.

By the time the sun was getting low and the three sat down to dinner, there were three steaming plates of fresh pasta in clam sauce, slices of a hearty, crusty bread to serve with them, and three glasses of a 2012 Vermentino white wine from Sardinia. Noah regaled them with tales of its origins.

"The real fun part," he was saying, his third glass having made him both apple-cheeked and enthusiastic about his subject, "is that no one knows how the grape got to Sardinia! In fact, no one knows where it's from. It's been used in France for centuries, and in Corsica of course, and in Liguria from the northwest of Italy, but Sardinia? It showed up in 1988, and no one knows how it got there. The first guy to make it, Vermentino di Sardegna, just showed up one day and started making it, and in 1996 Italy gave it a label."

As if to punctuate his point, Noah tossed back the last of his glass and reached for the bottle to pour himself a fourth. He knew that much wine sometimes had a strong effect on him, but screw it, he was having fun. Silvio Caravelli had proved to be interesting, knowledgeable, and on the fun-loving side, so it worked out well. What didn't work out was the fourth glass of wine, as he discovered the bottle to be empty.

Was that relief he saw on Christian's face? Nervous that he might be making a fool of himself, Noah leaned both hands on the table to stand up.

"Woah!" he said as he slipped a little and then sat back down. "Maybe I'd better switch to water."

"Probably a good idea," Christian said with a smile.

"You're so good to me, babe," Noah said, but then caught himself. Had he just given something away?

Sr. Caravelli laughed. "Indeed he is," the old man said, clapping a hand on Christian's back. "And a fine judge of character."

It warmed Noah's heart to hear that Silvio thought so, almost as much as it warmed his heart to see Christian stand up, go to the sink, and fill a tall water glass, which he brought back to Noah at the table. Christian kissed him on the top of his head as he set the glass down, and Noah could swear he saw the old man beaming.

Noah finished his water, and Christian and Silvio finished their wine, amid more discussion of Italian grapes and growers and vintners. Noah found that Christian's grandfather knew quite a bit, but he felt a touch of pride at knowing just a little bit more. He tried not to show off, no matter what the wine was telling him to do.

Finally he looked at the clock, judged his sobriety, and stood up.

"I should really be getting to bed," he said. "Busy day in the wine cellar tomorrow. Better start clearing the dishes."

"No, it's fine," Christian said a little too quickly. "I'll get it."

Noah, convinced this was a sign that he was probably swaying more than he thought he was, thanked Christian and wandered off to bed.

"THANKS, GRANDDAD," Christian said.

They were standing in the doorway to the villa, Christian leaning on the frame and his grandfather on the step facing him. The old man had watched, saying little, while Christian put the dishes away, rinsed off a few, and generally put the kitchen to rights. Or at least close enough that it wouldn't be a problem come morning.

"For what?" Silvio said innocently. "I did nothing. You had an old man over for dinner like a good grandson should."

"You know for what," Christian said, narrowing his eyes with a smile. "For being nice to Noah."

"Christian, what did I say to you?" his grandfather replied. "Your parents want you to be settled and happy, and I want you to be settled and happy. Not bouncing around Miami, not wandering back and forth between America and Italia like a transient, but happy. No matter what is happening with your mother and father right now, they both, like I, love you and want you to make your way in the world."

He sighed before continuing.

"This Noah is a good boy, I can tell. You choose wisely."

"I didn't choose him," Christian protested. "He just kind of fell into my lap."

Silvio shook his head. "These are details your grandfather does not need to hear."

"Granddad!"

The old man laughed. Christian laughed with him.

"He has a good head on his shoulders," he said to Christian. "He knows wine, he can cook, he has his goals... even if he doesn't know where they will lead." He alluded back to Noah's admission over dinner of what he had already told Christian, his uncertainty over where art history might take him.

"But it's clear that it is leading somewhere, and that's good. You could learn a lot from him."

"I'm not sure," Christian finally confessed. "Really? I mean, there are times when it feels like there's some kind of real connection between us, something that could mean a future, but there are other times when it feels so superficial. Like it's just a summer fling, something that happened because we were sharing a house, not for any other reason."

"Did your father ever tell you how he met your mother?"

Christian considered it. His parents, while they loved each other (or so he thought... hoped...), had never been overly romantic types. Christian was certain it had come up at some point, but damned if he could remember it. They had never been the types to swan around each other, telling it like a romantic bedtime story. A thought gave him a twinge of anxiety: if they were both more romantic, would they be closer together now?

"I'm not sure," he replied. "Probably? If so, I don't remember it."

His grandfather laughed. "Your father and I were hired to restore her family's house."

Christian grinned, almost laughing. "And let me guess, she was there that summer inspecting the wine?"

"Don't be foolish," the old man said. "She was inspecting the oil paintings."

He nodded politely to his grandson, a gesture of great respect from his elder as far as Christian was concerned, and began the trip back to the village.

Christian stared after the old man as he walked away, his mouth agog. *Is that... true? If so, is there, I don't know, fate?*

He shook his head, intent on not worrying about it. He had enough to concern him. As he made his final check around the villa, ascertaining whether the workmen had left things clean, making sure there weren't any doors standing open, and idly keeping an eye out for spiders, he wound up in the kitchen doing a more intense cleaning than he'd planned. He washed dishes that had merely been rinsed off, made a mental note to ask the plumber whether a dishwasher could be installed (a request the Cunninghams had hinted at but not said outright), and fretted over his relationship.

Noah had told him that if this was just a casual fling, he'd be fine with that, but Christian was starting to wonder whether he felt the same way. It occurred to him what a reversal this represented, based on what he knew of Noah's relationship history as compared to his own. In his own past, Christian had made a point of bouncing from one meaningless relationship to another, never wanting to get tied down. He'd always figured he had his whole life to meet "that special someone," and if he never did then that would be fine too.

What little Noah had told him about his own past made him sound like the opposite, as if he were the one likely to think about things like "a future" and "a serious relationship." But there he was, telling Christian that this casual thing, even if it was only for one summer, was fine.

His work in the kitchen done, Christian finally set out to do what he'd been putting off: finding out which room the slightly drunk Noah had decided to pass out in. He walked up to Noah's door and knocked lightly on it. There was no reply.

That meant Noah, whose adorable light snoring sometimes became louder when he'd had a few, was probably in Christian's bed. Hoping there would be no midnight run to the bathroom, Noah having mixed more than half a bottle of wine with a fresh clam sauce, he braced himself and turned the handle on his door.

There was Noah, not only still awake but obviously waiting for him. His lover sat upright, facing the door, his right arm leaned against the pillow and his left draped fetchingly across his stomach.

He was also obviously nude, Christian's white bedsheet resting across just his crotch and his lower leg, tempting him, teasing him. He could just make out a hint of Noah's brownish-red pubic hair peeking out above the edge of the sheet.

Noah smiled at him. "I thought you'd never come."

Christian smiled back. He peeled off his work clothes, and all doubt was banished from his mind as he jumped into that big, wonderful bed.

CHAPTER 14

"Hi, Mom."

"Noah! My darling baby!"

Noah gulped. He'd been putting off calling home. He loved his parents and they loved him, but their love could sometimes be a little… clingy.

"Don't mother the boy, Mary!" came his father's voice from the background.

"But I am his mother!" she replied.

"Hi, Dad," Noah said.

He was sitting at the desk in his room, the laptop set up in front of him, dealing with a sketchy internet connection's version of a video chat. His mother's face filled the screen, beaming from underneath her brown-rinse hairdo, and his father walked past in the background. He waved as he did, and Noah waved back.

"How's Tuscany? Ooh, you're getting a tan!"

Noah looked down at his own arms. It had been happening so gradually that he didn't even realize it, but his mom was right: his normally pale skin was darker than he was used to seeing it.

"Yeah! The summer sun here is beautiful. I wish you could see it. I emailed you some pictures. Did you get them?"

"We did, ooh la la!" his mother exclaimed. "That beautiful scenery, the hillsides, oh! I wish I'd done things like that when I was your age."

"Mom, you went to Washington in your wheelchair to protest for women's rights," Noah said. "You had adventures."

"Meh," his mother replied, waving off a lifetime of activism in the name of female reproductive justice and the disabled with a curt swish of her hand. "I guess. Anyway, tell me all about it! How's the food?"

"Actually, I do most of the cooking."

"Really? The whole of Tuscany, which includes Florence, by the way, and you couldn't find a decent chef?"

"I am a decent chef, Mom."

"Of course you are, sweetie, but you know what I mean."

"It's fine. The guy in charge of the renovations, Signor Caravelli, has an old woman come up from the village once a week with groceries for us. The Cunninghams weren't lying when they promised room and board."

"Well that's good at least. Tell me more about him, Caravelli. Is he easy to get along with? I remember when we had the family room redone. I know what a nightmare it is to be living in the house while there are renovations. Is it a nightmare, just you and this Italian gentleman?"

Noah realized at that moment exactly how much he'd really left out by not having called his parents since that one call, four weeks ago, to let them know he'd arrived safely. He wasn't certain how to get into Christian with them. His dad wouldn't care one way or the other, having made it clear that he had no interest in Noah's love life until there were engagement rings. Only then would he bother even meeting the guy. His mother, on the other hand…. If she knew that Christian and he were really hitting it off, she might start picking out engagement rings.

Biting his lip, uncertain how to proceed, he decided that no matter how his "summer romance" progressed, lying to his parents would only make things worse. He told his mother about how Sr. Caravelli had injured his leg before Noah had even arrived, and how his grandson had stepped in to do the renovations and repairs.

"His grandson?" his mother asked, one eyebrow raised.

"Yeah, his name's Christian." Noah hadn't thought that he'd given Christian's name any extra emphasis, but a mother's ears are sharper than their children know.

"Christian?" she asked, the eyebrow arching even higher.

"He's nice," Noah blurted out. He didn't want her to get the wrong idea, even though he realized that the idea she was forming wasn't far from the truth at all.

"I see," she said, in the tone of one who saw more than Noah would've wanted.

"It's not like...." He broke down. "Okay, it's exactly what you think!"

His mother made a noise that no human throat should be able to accommodate—somewhere between a squeal and an Amazonian cry of triumph. He had no doubt whatsoever that every dog in a three-block radius of their suburban Ohio home was now on its way over to his parents' house.

"Oh, sweetie!"

"Mom." Noah tried to be stern. "I don't want you to start imagining things. I'm having... let's call it a summer fling."

"Is he from Italy? Does he live there? Has he ever been to the States?"

Noah sighed. "He was born in Miami. He's here for the summer and so am I. It's proximity, that's all."

"When do we get to meet him? Or at least see him on the video?"

"Ideally never, Mother. Now look—" Suddenly the stern tone he'd been searching for came naturally, a thing he took as a sign that he meant business in a way he hadn't a moment ago. "Every relationship I've been in has fallen apart because I took it way too seriously way too soon. I'm not repeating my old mistakes. I like Christian and he likes me, but I made it clear to him, and I'm making it clear to you that I'm not planning out the rest of my life here. I'm having a nice summer. If it goes beyond that, I'll worry about it later."

Noah felt like he saw true understanding behind her eyes. It was an old argument between them. His mother was a born romantic, and he'd inherited a lot of that from her. It led to him diving in with both feet while the pool was still being filled, more than once. As much as he could see it pained her to do so, she nodded.

"Of course. You're absolutely right. Let me know how it goes."

She seemed tentative, as if not sure whether to keep talking. Noah rolled his eyes.

"Yes, I'll send a picture as soon as I can."

"Oh, it's not that," she said, shaking her head. "But yes, please do! No, it's some mail we got for you."

Noah furrowed his brow. While his apartment was sublet in New York City for the months he would be in Italy, his parents had graciously agreed to have his mail forwarded to them in Ohio. It was a little more than he normally asked of them, but it meant that there was no chance of something important going awry, like a financial statement or something else that might get his identity stolen. Brendan, the fellow student to whom he'd let the place, was only reliable about rent because his family handled it for him. Noah didn't trust him to keep the mail around until he got home.

What could be that important?

"What is it?" he asked.

"It's from school," she said. Off camera, Noah's mother rummaged around a bit through some papers but eventually held up a slim envelope. It was definitely from NYU. It had his address on it, the yellow forwarding sticker from the post office, and big block letters saying URGENT INFORMATION REGARDING FUNDING. PLEASE OPEN AT ONCE.

Noah gulped.

"I didn't want to open your mail," his mother told him, "but I figured we'd better chat soon so I could tell you about it. Should I... I don't know, forward it to you there?"

He had no idea how long it would take to reach the small Tuscan village that served as the nearest post office box. Days? Weeks? After he'd left to go home, maybe? He couldn't take that chance.

"No, I think you'd better just open it," he said. "Do you mind doing it now?" It was a little late in Ohio, thanks to the six-hour time difference, and he didn't want to demand, but he also had no doubt that with even a miniscule amount of prodding, his mother would do so.

"Of course, let me get a letter opener just in case," his mother said, rummaging around off camera. Noah heard paper tearing and then his mother reappeared, holding the unfolded single sheet of paper.

"It says... oh my!" she gasped, holding one hand to her mouth.

"Don't keep the boy in suspense, Mary!" came his father's voice from off camera. So Dad was still lurking around nearby. Noah suppressed a laugh.

"It's from the Nelson people! I'm sorry, Melton, the people at Melton!"

Noah's eyes got wide. "Melton" was short for the Melton Foundation for Print Arts. They were behind one of the grants that he'd applied for earlier, a grant that would fund his work for at least a year, maybe more. It even came with opportunities for study at places like the Met or the Museum of Modern Art, or abroad at the Louvre or elsewhere. It was a prestigious grant that would open doors behind the scenes and allow access to resources most mere graduate students could never hope to acquire on their own.

For a moment he dared to hope, before reminding himself why he'd applied in the first place. He'd had several glasses of very cheap Pinot Noir and let his best friend talk him into the application. There was no way he'd been approved, a thing he'd known even as he was sending the form in.

"You can give me the bad news, Mom," he said. "I know that good news would've come in a thicker envelope."

"No, you got it!" she said.

Noah's jaw dropped. "You're... you're kidding."

"I'm not!" She turned the paper around, facing it to his screen, and pointed wildly at the typed letter, even though it was far too close to the camera for him to read.

"Read it to me!" he said.

"Dear applicant, we are pleased to inform you... yadda yadda yadda...."

"Mother!"

When he finally got her to accept that every word might be important, she broke down and read the whole thing to him word for word. The grant, and the esteem that went with it, was impressive. As soon as he got home, at the beginning of the next semester, parts of it would kick in right away. He would need to submit a formal proposal detailing his intended course of study and his uses for the money, but that was no problem. He had been required to submit several possible options as part of the application process so he could just revisit one of those if he had to. The letter made it clear that he wasn't required to use any of those, and furthermore that they had been so impressed by the submissions that they were willing to entertain options where he threw them out the window entirely!

Noah had to take another breath. Not only would he be able to basically set his own course when it came to period and method of study, but the money would be enough that he could quit his job. He wouldn't have to be a sommelier after all!

That thought turned his mind back to Christian. Sweet Christian, whose eyes could be either puppy-dog or bedroom-sultry from moment to moment, and who seemed like he really cared about Noah. Christian, who would undoubtedly be stuck renovating the villa long after Noah was back in New York doing whatever he ended up doing with his fancy new grant money.

"Oh, baby, isn't that wonderful?" his mother cried. "The answer to all your worries!"

Noah put on a brave face. He brushed thoughts of Christian to the back of his mind. He still had another month to worry about that. Live in the moment, right?

He agreed with his mother that it was, indeed, amazing, and stayed on the line while his father came over to congratulate him as well. After which he begged off, saying he had to go start dinner.

By the time dinner rolled around, Christian was ready to eat like a goddamn bear. It had been a hell of a day. While Noah was fooling around on the computer, coming up from the wine cellar just once to hang out in his own room for a while, Christian had helped the workers lay the final foundations at the outdoor patio. It had been hard, heavy work under the hot Tuscan sun, and while Christian was proud of his muscled physique and never one to shy away from hard work, he wondered as he washed his hands for dinner whether that day had been a little much for him.

The villa was coming along very, very nicely, he had to admit. The guest rooms were basically finished, the kitchen and master bedroom had both been more or less done before the workmen even arrived, and the only things left in the pool area were decorative like the tiling. As he ticked off the to-do list it occurred to him that the same was true for most of what was left. The additional rooms like the study and the library were in fine shape in terms of structure, electricity, and plumbing. They just needed to be totally renovated, which he told himself would be his pleasure to do over the next four weeks.

He was developing an unexpected sense of pride in his work, as well as his body. He'd read novels and nonfiction in college written by "working class heroes" and about "men who found fulfillment in labor," but he'd always laughed it off. Now that it was a part of his daily life, he felt it taking on new significance.

"What's for dinner?" he asked Noah as he walked into the kitchen.

"Steaks," Noah replied, flipping one over to sear. "I had a taste for it. Hope you don't mind."

Christian stepped up behind Noah and folded his arms around his lover's waist, relishing with unmixed glee the way Noah leaned back into him in reply.

"I'll take your meat any way you give it, baby," he said.

"Perv."

"Sexy."

"I'm cooking." Noah said it with a little chuckle, lightly slapping the one hand of Christian's that had started to drift below the waist. Christian let go but gave a good slap on the ass as he walked away. He began to pick out plates and glasses, but out of the corner of his eye, he was gratified to see Noah smile.

When the steaks were done, Noah served, then directed Christian's hand to a modest Barolo he had pulled from the cellar. Christian didn't always understand when Noah talked about how the "full-bodied red" would bring out the "depth" of the sauce and the "piquancy" of the peppercorns, but he listened attentively anyway. Whether he understood it or not, listening to Noah talk about his subject was a pleasure all its own (and more than a little sexy). As they sat down to eat, he took Noah's hand in his.

"I don't want to get weird or mushy or anything," he said, "but this has been on my mind for too long, and I gotta say it. This last month has been one of the best of my life, and I'm excited for the month to come."

Noah smiled but tensed a little, so Christian quickly shifted to put his mind at ease.

"I know, I know, no future talk. That's not what I'm saying. Just that if this is all there is... I want you to know that I really love all that this is."

In response, Noah leaned across the table and kissed him. It tasted of red wine and of spices, and Christian, though usually no romantic, couldn't shake the feeling that the kiss was somehow special. That it wasn't one of their "segue to sex" kisses, neither was it a "cuddling in the early morning" kiss (which Noah had a sickeningly sweet tendency to deliver on Christian's nose). It was filled with passion but somehow... not passionate? As their lips drifted apart, Christian decided he'd be happiest if he told himself that it was love.

He smiled. "What was that for?"

"For being you," Noah said, cutting into the steak. "For respecting me and how I... need things to be."

Christian decided that maybe he could get away with a little gentle prodding. "Can I ask why you need things to be a certain way?"

Noah looked at him, smiling but sad somehow. "I just...," Noah began, then faltered as he considered his words. "Let me put it like this. Every relationship I've been in, I've been the one to ruin it. I jump in with both feet, going from flirting to rom-com in the space of a week or so. I've pushed away a lot of good people, at least a few of which I think might've stayed if I'd let things run their course. And… I like you."

Christian brightened at the thought. He waggled one eyebrow.

"Horndog. Don't go making everything a joke," Noah scolded him, his tone playful but clear: *I am opening up here.* Christian wiped the look off his face and waited for Noah to finish chewing a bite of steak.

"I do, Christian. I do like you. And I don't want to ruin this by thinking it's something it's not, or worse, by forcing it to be something it's not. We're having fun. Let's keep having fun. Let's keep playing house… and occasionally doctor."

"Oh, so you get to make sexy jokes but I don't?"

Noah laughed, and Christian was overjoyed to see it.

"This summer's going to end, Christian. We both know that. Let's find out what happens after that… when it's after that, okay?"

"Hey." Christian shrugged. "You're talking to Mr. No Strings here. I'll be honest too: I hope there's an 'after that.' But if there isn't, then I won't hold it against you."

Christian's breath caught in his throat. How had he let a thing like that slip out? The only thing that kept him from panicking was Noah, raising his wineglass.

"I'll drink to that," he said.

Their glasses clinked, and talk turned to the renovation and its progress, but on the inside, Christian's fears didn't go away so easily.

CHAPTER 15

AS CHRISTIAN prattled on about how he and the contractors were choosing what type of wood had to go in the library, Noah sipped his wine nervously. He'd been on the verge of telling Christian everything: about the grant money, about how no matter how much 'fun' they were having, they would almost certainly be parting at the end of the summer. The Melton money didn't require him to be in New York necessarily but he'd at least need to be there to make his proposal. And when he thought about the museums, the galleries, the influential people...all of the ones he knew were back in the Big Apple. There was no way around it: he'd have to leave Christian behind.

The only thing that kept him from just blurting it out was the realization that it would've put an unshakable pall over their remaining weeks together, and he wanted those weeks to be the best they could possibly be. For both of them.

With that in mind, when dinner was done, he made a spur-of-the-moment suggestion on a whim, a departure from routine.

"Now that the patio's done, is the furniture set up?" he asked. "Wanna go look at the stars?"

Christian's grin was all the answer he needed, so they cleared the table and rinsed the dishes and headed outside. It was a beautiful night. The nearby village produced almost no light pollution, and the villa was far enough from the nearest major city, Florence, that the view of the stars was magnificent. Noah had seen it before, more than once since coming to the villa, but he'd never really stopped to take it all in. And never with Christian.

The two sat on a love seat, out under the stars but for a canvas umbrella that hung overheard nearby in case it started to rain. The idea was preposterous, there wasn't a cloud in the sky, but summer showers weren't unknown. The love seat was wicker but heavily cushioned for comfort. Noah couldn't escape the fact that it really didn't fit in with the rest of the "Italiana rusticana" aesthetic, which was odd because Eloise Cunningham had picked out the rest of the furniture with exquisite taste. He was forced to conclude that the odd-looking but extremely comfortable outdoor love seat was one of Mr. Cunningham's additions.

The view was magnificent, and the presence of a big, warm Christian right next to him as the night turned colder after sunset was the only thing that made it better. Noah thought for a moment how nice it would be to just cuddle in close, allowing Christian to drape his arm around him.

Unexpectedly, before Noah could move, Christian did exactly that but in reverse. The slightly larger man leaned over, putting his head on Noah's shoulder with a sigh, and almost by instinct Noah raised his arm to wrap it around Christian's shoulders. His well-muscled lover curled up against him, as much as the love seat would allow, and Noah realized that this was even better than what he had imagined the alternative would be like. Christian's skin was still warm, both from natural body heat and from the day's labors, and the muscles of his neck and shoulders just below that skin were relaxed but firm.

It was just as he was really starting to enjoy the moment, dreading its inevitable conclusion, when he felt something tap lightly against his shirt just below Christian's head. A little bug, maybe? Lost in the outdoors and seeking heat? Was Christian poking him? It was too light for that. It happened again.

Christian sat up, and it was immediately evident to Noah what had happened. Christian was crying.

"I'm sorry," he said, wiping his eyes with the back of his hand. "I just... there's a lot going on right now."

"So tell me about it," Noah replied, unable to keep his voice from expressing his genuine concern.

Christian waved him off. "Nah, it's cool. I don't want to dump stuff on you. Keeping it casual, right?"

Noah's care for Christian drove him to press harder... as did his curiosity. "Casual is one thing, but if we agreed that we're going to do this for a summer, then we're going to do it all the way. It's not me, is it? I mean, if it is and you don't want to talk about it, then I—"

"No!" Christian said, a little too loud. "No, it's not you at all. It's... it's my folks. Dad reached out to my granddad for help getting an annulment. I just found out when he was here yesterday."

"Oh." Noah didn't know what to say, how to offer advice or to help. Since Christian had first mentioned the potential divorce he had felt awkward because it just wasn't something he knew how to address. His own parents were so close, even after all these years, he really couldn't picture what it would feel like to have the rug pulled out from under you quite so hard.

So he did the only thing that made sense. He wrapped his arm around Christian's big shoulders once more and pulled him back in, trying to signal to the other man that he could talk or cry or do whatever he needed to do.

"It's just, like," he said, "I don't know what to do. If they split up, I don't know what happens to me. I feel like such a baby even saying that, like I'm reliant on them for everything, but the truth is that I am. I live in their house, I eat their food, I drive my mom's second car, and my dad pays my credit card bills. Not like you, you're so self-reliant."

Noah's eyebrows went up. He had really never thought of himself that way. When he considered it, he supposed it was true. He really only ever leaned on his parents for things like money if he had no other choice.

"Do you have a job at home?" Noah asked.

Christian was silent.

"I mean, you said you work for your dad flipping houses, right? Surely you could ask him to start paying you. You'd still be dependent on him, but you could get your own place and all that."

"I could," Christian acknowledged. "Or I could just stay here. Dad and Granddad both say I have all the right things to get dual citizenship. I could just live here, working for Granddad. But that's not the problem."

He sat up to face Noah, and while he hadn't felt any more droplets, Noah could tell that Christian had continued to cry. His eyes were red, and there were a few wet streaks down his face. He wiped it all away before he went on, but Noah could still see the signs.

"I feel like such a baby," he repeated. "Such a little kid complaining about all this. There are people out there with real problems, and here I am trying to decide between a career in renovation in Miami or a career in renovation in Italy."

He gave a short, self-deprecating laugh, but Noah didn't laugh with him.

"I get it," Noah said. "It's a lot of stress. No matter what happens, your life is going to get flipped upside down, and even if the options are good ones, it's a big step that you're going to have to make sooner than you wanted to."

Christian nodded.

"Christian, I mean this, I really do, so I want to make sure you hear me say it." Noah took a deep breath. "And I'm not just saying it because I care about you, okay?"

Christian didn't reply.

"You're good at what you do. Maybe you don't see it, or haven't seen it, but I have and I do. Every day. You know all the ins and outs of this house. You know what has to be done where and when and how. I don't know if it's from studying American building codes or Italian ones, but you're not any less self-reliant than I am. You have different skills than mine, not any lesser."

"Thanks."

"I mean it."

"I know you do, and I mean thanks." Christian wiped his eyes.

"Was this... was this why you wanted to talk about our relationship?" Noah asked. "Or at least about me. Were you feeling me out because you were worried about your own future?"

Christian laughed for real this time, and Noah smiled with him.

"Yeah, I guess it was," he said. "It hadn't occurred to me, but you're probably right. I don't want to put any pressure on you, but I've really enjoyed these last few weeks, and it was just kind of nice to imagine... to imagine that if I had to land somewhere, you might be there with me."

"That's the sweetest thing I've ever heard," Noah said, and he meant it. Deep inside, though, the low simmer of worry about going home to New York and deciding what to do with the Melton grant was turning up to a boil. The hard truth was that if he wanted to make the most out of that money, then he'd have a tough time coming up with a project anywhere other than New York City.

Christian smiled and leaned forward to kiss Noah, which Noah allowed. It wasn't much longer before they retired for the evening, the romantic baring of souls leading not to an extended romp between the sheets but to the two of them, under their covers, holding each other against the dark of the night as both drifted off to sleep.

THE NEXT two weeks went by quickly for Christian, almost too quickly when he found the time to stop and think about it. Noah was as sweet (and frisky) as ever, and their routine held up even through tribulations like the time one of the workmen almost flooded the kitchen from the pool, but Christian couldn't escape the feeling that something had changed between them that night. Noah seemed distant sometimes, often visibly shaking himself out of it as if he were pondering something he didn't want to admit even to himself. Christian assumed that Noah, like him, was thinking ahead to the looming end of their two months together.

With only two further weeks remaining to the amount of time Noah was guaranteed to be in Tuscany, Christian accidentally overheard the conversation that would change everything.

He had let the workmen go home early since it was Friday and most had plans. The progress that day had been outstanding so Christian was feeling charitable. He was just about to knock on Noah's door when he heard voices coming from inside. Noah's was clear, but the other was a little tinny, as if Noah were video chatting with the US again. It was only after a moment that he realized the identity of the second voice.

"No, sir, it's right on schedule," Noah was saying.

"Fine, just fine," came the voice of Chester Cunningham. "Better than fine, in fact. These sheets you've sent look outstanding. Mrs. Cunningham is the real wine expert, but I know how to read a spreadsheet, and the work is very impressive. Do you think you'll be done early?"

Christian realized that he was eavesdropping and that he should walk away, but if it was just the Cunninghams, then what was the harm? The desire to hear what else was said only deepened when he heard Noah hesitate before responding.

"I mean, I guess I could if that's really important to you, Mr. Cunningham," Noah said. "I could try and wrap it all up. I had kind of counted on having all of the time, though, you know."

Christian's heart felt like it had skipped a beat.

"Then take your time!" said the ever-boisterous Chester Cunningham, and Christian could breathe again. "There's no rush. I just thought it wouldn't hurt to ask. Won't hurt your paycheck any, if that was your worry."

"I appreciate that, sir," Noah replied. "But I'd like to finish the job as fully as possible."

"I like a man who finishes what he starts. By the way, I heard that you got a special something in the mail a few weeks ago."

Special something? Christian wondered. He still felt bad spying on Noah's conversation, but he had gone too far to stop now. He didn't know of Noah receiving any mail while he'd been at the villa, certainly not a package or something like that. Just the emails from his parents that he mentioned from time to time.

"Mr. Cunningham, how—how did you find out about that?"

"Find out about it? Who do you think put in a good word for you?" was Chester Cunningham's reply. "Mrs. Cunningham and I are on the Melton board, and we like to be good to the people who are good to us. Your professor said your schoolwork is excellent, and between that and what you've done for us at the villa, we thought the least we could do was say a few nice words to the grant committee."

"I-I really don't know what to say!"

"Well, 'thank you' would be appropriate," he heard Cunningham tease.

"Thank you!"

"Heh. Now don't go doubting yourself or anything. You got in on your own merits. But in the world today, sometimes even the most deserving don't get their just reward without a little kick from those who've gone before. Do you have plans for how you're going to use the grant? The board will be very excited to hear your proposal once you're stateside again. All of New York City, or even the world lies before you!"

Christian couldn't believe what he was hearing. At last he felt like he finally knew what Noah saw when he pictured his own future.

"To be perfectly honest, sir, I hadn't put a lot of thought into it yet. All of the potential proposals I submitted are intriguing to me, but I do want to come up with something original as well. The truth is that I've been concentrating on my work here, but yes, it is nice to know there's something big waiting for me back home."

"Something big? Something life-changing!" Cunningham boomed. "Previous recipients have gone on to great things, and I'm sure I expect nothing less from you!"

"You're very kind, sir."

"Excellent, just excellent. While we have the call open, I do want to ask one small favor. Is that other fellow there? The Caravelli boy who's overseeing the work while his grandfather's laid up? He sent me a few quotes I'd like to discuss with him."

"I'm sure he's around here somewhere, Mr. Cunningham. Let me go grab him."

Christian's eyes went wide when he realized he was about to get caught. At the last second he broke out of his worried reverie, fretting over Noah having definite New York City plans at the end of the summer and not even telling him, and bolted for his own room. It was all he could do to lie down on the bed, fully clothed, before he heard Noah calling down the hallway for him.

"In here!" he answered back, using every trick from cardio exercises to slow his breathing back to normal speed.

"Hey, babe," Noah said on entering, smiling at Christian. "Where is everyone?"

For a moment Christian couldn't even focus on the other man's words. Why would they talk about the workmen at a time like this? He snapped out of it as fast as he was able.

"Uh, I sent 'em home early. They worked hard today. We all did. Early dinner? Or do you have wine stuff to do still?"

"Nothing that won't keep. I was video calling with Mr. Cunningham, updating him, and he asked if he could talk to you. Should I... tell him I couldn't find you?"

Christian chuckled. "Nah, I'll talk to him. Is he on your laptop?"

Noah nodded. "Sign it all out and turn it off when you're done, please. I'll go start dinner."

Christian walked to the door, where Noah waited to give him a little kiss before they separated. Then he headed into Noah's room while he watched Noah walk down the hall toward the kitchen.

The conversation with Cunningham was brief and purely professional. He had some technical questions about bids for the pool tilework, input on the new wood for the library, nothing Christian couldn't handle. But the whole time he had a sinking feeling he couldn't shake: the fear that, for as much as Chester Cunningham seemed to respect him as a renovator and contractor, he would never have gone out on a limb for him the way he had for Noah. Despite the differences between them that often fit like a yin and a yang, it was a reminder of the fact that he and Noah really were from two different worlds.

What did I think was going to happen? he rebuked himself as the call ended and he stepped into Noah's bathroom to wash up for dinner. *A guy like Noah would come live with me in Miami? In my parents' house? My divorcing parents' house? Or that he might want me with him in New York, where he'd do all the art stuff and I'd probably end up working construction?*

Again he chastised himself. For one thing, he had come to enjoy working with his hands more than he'd ever thought he might. Like Noah had said, it wasn't a skill to look down on, it was just different. Furthermore, he had to remember not to talk to Noah about "their future together." That was how Noah wanted it, and he was determined to respect Noah's wishes, but it was going to be tough.

Both men were quiet during dinner. Noah twirled a fork through some spaghetti, and Christian almost complimented his improving skill at pasta making but thought better of it.

"I didn't—"

"If you could—"

Both laughed as they spoke at the same time. Noah gestured with his fork first. "Go ahead."

Christian sighed. "I didn't mean to, but I overheard your conversation with Cunningham. The end of it, anyway."

Noah's eyes narrowed, then went wider. "Oh."

"He said you got a grant," Christian went on. "'Life-changing' were his words."

"You heard that."

Christian nodded.

Noah took a deep breath, then a sip of the truly delightful Pinot Blanco he'd picked out for the meal, and set his glass back down.

"I applied before I came here. Way before I'd even gotten this job offer, let alone before I met you. It's enough money that I won't have to wait tables. I'm very excited."

"You don't sound excited."

"Well I'm not sorry about it, that's for sure," Noah scoffed.

119

"Who said you should be sorry?" Christian spat back. "You're good at what you do. I'm happy and proud for you!"

"Okay then!"

They ate in silence a moment more before both started to laugh at the ridiculousness of their little shouting match.

"I'm sorry."

"No, I'm sorry."

They ate some more before Christian spoke again.

"So what kind of a grant is it? Scholarship for NYU or something?"

"Kind of," Noah said, taking another sip of the wine to swallow a mouthful of pasta with. "More like independent study. They give the grant to graduate level students in the arts, like me, who have proposals for specialized work they want to do that no one's ever done before. Real definitive studies."

"What's your proposal about?"

Noah shrugged. "I had to submit three of them as part of the application process. I think they're all interesting, which is good because I'll probably end up stuck with one of them, but to be honest. none of them, y'know, light my soul on fire."

"What does light your soul on fire, then?"

Noah gave Christian a big, exaggerated wink and Christian laughed out loud.

"Well, I'm not posing nude for any art or anything like that," he said. "But you can study me all you like."

That made it Noah's turn to laugh. "No, I think naked Christian Caravelli is something I'd like to keep in my private collection for a while."

Noah took Christian's hand. Christian felt the difference in that hand, once soft and almost delicate but now rougher, manly. Not calloused like his was becoming as he spent weeks doing the much more intense labor that Noah wasn't, but somehow... stronger.

"This... this is exactly what I didn't want," Noah said, laughing nervously as he wiped away the beginnings of tears with his other hand. "The next two weeks might be all we have together. The grant is an opportunity I just can't pass up."

"I wouldn't want you to," Christian interjected.

"So if the next two weeks might be it, I didn't want to spend them worried about the looming end date hanging over our heads."

"All right," Christian allowed. "I get that. But can I make a request?"

"Of course."

Christian took a deep breath. "I don't know if what's pulling us together is unique to this place, these circumstances. If we'd just met randomly on the streets of New York, would we have what we have right now? Maybe, maybe not. But I hope that we would've, that we would still be compatible. I understand not wanting to have that conversation now. Can you promise me that we will have it one day? That when the day comes, you won't just say goodbye?"

"I promise," Noah said, and they sealed it with a kiss. Dinner went on, and wrapped up, and another night was had stargazing before going to bed. Christian couldn't shake, however, the feeling that something had irrevocably changed. That something was lost or broken, and that it might not be repaired in time.

CHAPTER 16

NOAH AWOKE to what was becoming a heart-breakingly common sensation: the feel of Christian, still sleeping, with an arm wrapped around him. It had been a few days since their tentative conversation about the future, and Christian had kept his promise about giving Noah space. Noah planned to keep his promise in return that the conversation was only delayed, not cancelled.

Whenever that warm body was wrapped around him, though, thoughts of ever leaving the villa vanished from his mind. There had been a few days when the summer heat had been so bad that he'd simply pushed the other man off because he was sweating too badly, but most of the time he just enjoyed the closeness so much that he clung to Christian while both their bodies grew slick from perspiration.

He took a moment to consider how much the summer had changed him. He wouldn't have called himself shy—no one who wears Speedos competitively in high school and college has big hang-ups about showing off their body—but his discomfort in casual settings had been completely wiped away. Whereas before he'd have worn a T-shirt and boxers to bed in even the warmest of weather, he reflected on his nude body pressed against Christian's and how normal it had become.

When a certain part of sleeping Christian's anatomy pressed hard against the small of Noah's back, another thing that happened fairly often, he smiled. He thought back fondly on the memory of that first awkward sexual encounter, but that train of thought was headed for a very melancholy station. Avoid it though he might, he couldn't ignore the fact that it all might be coming to an end.

Melton had emailed him directly. They were polite, almost effusive, but clear on one point: they needed an answer. Accept or reject, and if accept then what was the plan to use the money? His ideas for the money needed some work, but as far as acceptance, he unfortunately knew what his answer would have to be.

"What're you thinking about?" came the voice from behind him, and Noah flinched.

"I didn't think you were awake."

"Mm-hmm, I'm here all right," Christian replied. Noah could see in his mind's eye the smile on his lover's face. He reached around behind him and took hold of Christian's substantial erection.

"Did you want to do something about this?" he asked, trying to keep his tone playful and light.

Christian growled at him. "I'd love to, but I can't. The tile guy's coming early today to look at the pool. I gotta hop in the shower, like, now."

Quickly, mischievously, Noah ripped the sheet away and flung it onto the floor, exposing both of their sweaty naked bodies to the cool morning air. "Then let's hit the showers."

"Gah!" Christian reacted, instinctively reaching for the sheet before accepting his fate and flopping back on the bed. "Sadist."

"You wish."

A shower and a light breakfast later and they were off to their separate corners again, Christian ready to greet his tile specialist and Noah grabbing his laptop and heading for the wine cellar. His work really was nearing completion, and putting on the finishing touches had been a nice distraction to keep him from getting into a funk around Christian and spoiling their good time. The database of his catalog was complete, and very thorough, he was proud to say. Each bottle had an entry that described the vintage, the point of origin (as best he could tell), the rough dollar value on the current market (again, as best he could tell), basic care instructions for whoever they hired to care for the collection when he was gone, and just for extra credit, a tagged and searchable field for what sorts of dishes to pair it with.

Out of both a desire to be thorough and the thought of a little something extra for going above and beyond, Noah had even taken pictures of each bottle. Some of the photos weren't great because the vintages themselves were so old that he didn't want to expose them to bright light, but he paired his pictures up with the corresponding database entry so there could be no confusion. The artwork on some of the labels was magnificent, though, older ones looking like they'd been done by hand. He knew he'd keep digital copies of the best pictures on his laptop long after going home, for his personal art collection.

There was that thought again, he realized as it floated back to the top of his mind. *Going home.*

He shook himself just a little, just enough to shake the thought off and concentrate. What he *hadn't* done was organize as he went. He knew roughly where each bottle was, but they were all mixed together. Whoever had come before him did a real number on this place, seemingly just putting bottles in randomly as new ones were acquired, and Noah planned to spend the next week organizing.

The final week, he realized, the thought bobbing up again like a bad penny. The truth, he considered, was that he was just avoiding the inevitable. If he did care for Christian, and he believed he did, then it was time to tell him that the point of no return was at last in sight.

At dinner he braced himself. And then, holding back tears with every ounce of strength, he opened his mouth.

"I'm going back to New York."

Christian stopped eating but did not look up right away. He took a drink of their wine for the evening, a Chardonnay that Noah had chilled to serve with the seared salmon, and then finally looked up.

"So that's it? That's the discussion?"

"Not all of it I hope," Noah said. "But that's how it ends, yeah. I… I really do feel something for you, Christian. I hesitate to call it love after only two months, but I admit that it's strong. This really is a once in a lifetime opportunity for me, though. If you feel something back for me, then I hope you'd want me to take advantage of it."

Christian was quiet, but his expressive eyes spoke volumes. He looked away, and when he looked back, the tears had already begun.

"Noah, of course," he said. "Of course I want you to take it, and I want it to be amazing for you. But that doesn't mean I'm not sad about it."

Noah felt his own tears and tried hard to will them away.

"Your life is in New York," Christian continued. "I understand."

"You could come with me. It could be *our* life in New York."

Christian shook his head. "Your life is there, mine is here. I have to get this house finished, and what would I do in New York? Construction? Be one of a million guys trying to lift things for a living? Or one of ten million trying to make use of a communications degree?"

Noah rolled his eyes at Christian's self-deprecation. "I hate that you put yourself down about that. You have a college degree. Not everybody does."

Christian shrugged but said nothing. Noah reached across the table and took his hand.

"I don't want this to be the end, I really don't. Can we try across the distance, at least for a little while?"

Christian looked at him skeptically. "I've... I've done long distance before, Noah. I don't know. It's not easy."

"If it was easy, then everyone would do it."

"Fair enough, but I'm still not convinced. Do we want to go into the clichés? How we're 'not like the rest' and 'our love is strong enough to stand the test of distance' and crap like that?"

Noah opened his mouth to deliver a sharp retort but then closed it again. Completely unplanned, he smiled instead.

"As a matter of fact, I think it is, Christian. We were brought together once. I believe we can stay together any way we have to until we can be together physically again."

Christian, who looked as if he too had been ready for an argument, broke into a similar smile.

"If you're game I'm game," he said. Christian squeezed Noah's hand, and Noah squeezed back.

CHRISTIAN MADE an effort not to speak of it any further. They exchanged email addresses and phone numbers so it would be already done when the day finally came, and that was that. It made Christian nervous, having tried cross-country relationships a few times before and it not working out. It was especially hard to remain optimistic as he pictured going intercontinental, but every day (and every night) reminded him that their love was strong. They had a chance.

An idea did come to him of how he could give Noah a bit of a send-off. He filed that away for later.

Despite the poignancy that entered their regular routine of cohabitation, eating together, and nights of either tender romance or strenuous sport-fucking, Christian's workdays actually grew easier and easier. The villa was coming along well. He had no doubt that he'd still be working on it after Noah was gone. He estimated that he probably had another month ahead of him. But it was all finishing touches. The tiling professional had offered a fair quote for the pool and had begun his work with Christian's help. A team was being arranged, but no contracts had been signed, which left Christian to start the project of laying down tiles by himself. If he didn't at least get started, then it could throw the whole schedule out of whack, and he was proud of the Caravelli contracting family delivering on schedule. So far.

The Cunninghams had approved the installation of better lighting and humidity and temperature controls in the wine cellar, with some input from Noah as to their needs, and Christian had a guy lined up. He was waiting for Noah to leave so that his hire wouldn't be in the way, but it pained him to think of "anticipating" the day Noah was gone.

These were the thoughts going through Christian's mind one cloudy afternoon as he worked on the pool tiles when a voice behind him startled him.

"You really have good hands for the work, you know."

"Gah!" he cried, wheeling around sharply and dropping everything. The trowel, covered in tile mortar, went flying out of his right hand, and the pale blue ceramic tile he'd been about to place went flying out of his left. A split second into its flight, his eyes grew wide with the realization of what had just happened: those tiles were absurdly expensive.

Lunging forward with the speed and athleticism that had marked his college career, Christian made a bold dive across the empty pool for the tile. It bounced off one of the fingers on his left hand, then his right, bobbling like crazy in midair as he tried to grab it. Finally, in a desperate move, he intentionally overextended himself and wrapped all five fingers of his left hand all the way around it. The decorative pool tile, thirty dollars apiece, was safe in his grasp.

Christian himself, however, went crashing down onto the bottom of the pool.

"Granddad!"

"This is how you speak to your elder?" Silvio asked in reply. "Stop fumbling about in an empty pool, my boy, and get up here. I'm ready to inspect your progress."

Christian stood up, and his grandfather made an exasperated sound and rolled his eyes. He looked down. As was common on workdays when he wasn't expecting company, Christian wore only his short cutoff jeans. Not only were they a little tight around the hips, but at some point during his fall, the top button seemed to have popped right off and they'd slid a few inches down. The tightness around the hips was the only reason he was flashing his grandfather a view of pubic hair rather than something a little more personal.

"And this is how you *dress* for your elder?" Silvio waved a hand as he walked into the house proper. "Madonna mia, holy mother, let the Cunninghams never know that these boys turned their villa into a house of—"

"Enough, Granddad!" Christian shouted. He placed the tile gently on the stack of other tiles where it belonged, tucked every part of himself back into place where it belonged, and climbed out of the pool.

The tour he gave his grandfather was much like every other inspection, though even more cursory. Silvio Caravelli nodded at this item and that, asking a few questions but always pleased with Christian's explanations. It ended where it began, back at the pool.

"Why are you doing the tiling then, boy?" Silvio asked. He pointed with his cane at the spot where he'd found his grandson working. "You do a fine job, but is this not why we hired men?"

"Granddad," Christian began patiently, "we talked about this. The tiling expert laid out the plan, but I've been having trouble finding a group that can do it. The workmen that were doing the rest of the house refused to touch it, something about their insurance not covering something like this. So the expert gave me the plan and I'm working on it until we get a signed contract."

Silvio smacked himself in the forehead.

"Si, si, of course. Your grandfather's not what he once was, and it is good you're here. So you are finding a contract group?"

Christian nodded. "Until then, it's just me."

Silvio leaned forward, out over the edge of the pool, squinting as if to inspect the work up close. Christian stepped closer to him, worried for a moment that his grandfather might lean over too far and forget that the pool had no water in it.

"If you want to see it closer, Granddad, maybe go around to the other side of the pool and kneel down?"

"No, no, I don't need to make trouble," the old man said. "You don't use too much of the stucco, do you, the mortar? And you use a level to keep it all even and neat?"

"Of course, Granddad."

"Show me."

"Why?"

"Because you'll face the business end of this cane, that's why!" Silvio said. "First you throw tiles around the pool then practically flash me, I swear."

Christian sighed. Gingerly he stepped down the concrete steps into the pool and headed for the area he'd been working at. His grandfather followed him around the outside of the pool and knelt by that same area, exactly as Christian had suggested, but of course without any hint of recognition that it had been a good idea.

So under the hawklike eyes of his grandfather, Christian got back to work. He soon found himself in that zone again, laying the mortar, laying the tile, measuring, cleaning, applying sealant to protect against water and then moving on. By the time Silvio broke his reverie, he'd done almost an entire horizontal row of the small four-inch-by-four-inch tiles.

"Very nice, very nice indeed," the old man said, reaching over the pool's side to run his hand along the younger Caravelli's work. "My boy, when you first came to spend the summer at your old grandfather's house, did you ever imagine you'd be doing something like this?"

"Actually I was pretty sure I'd spend the summer chasing cute Italian guys around Florence."

"Bah!" Silvio waved that suggestion away. "A waste of your time. Look at what you've done here, with trowel and level and your hands. You've done the work of at least three men, and you've done a job superb. You should be proud."

Christian stepped back to admire what he had done under his grandfather's watchful eye. Truth be told, he found that he was proud.

Noah's going to love swimming in this—

The thought broke off while still half-formed. Noah wasn't going to love swimming in this pool. Even the most optimistic estimates didn't have it as finished before he would be going home to New York.

"Is everything all right?" his grandfather suddenly asked. "Is there something wrong between you and—"

"I'd rather not talk about it," Christian said. "Thanks, Granddad."

For once, possibly for the first time, the old man respected his privacy. He nodded and said no more on the subject. They made an agreement that in a few weeks time they would check in once again, and he reiterated his faith in Christian's ability to pick the right tile workers and sign the best contract. Then he was gone, leaving Christian alone with his thoughts all afternoon.

"What're you thinking about for the grant?" Christian asked Noah that night. Again, they were on the patio staring up at the stars.

Noah looked at him with a furrowed brow. "I thought you didn't want to talk about it?"

Christian thought back to his conversation with his grandfather. Putting things off wasn't a way of handling them.

"Do I want to think about the day you're leaving me?" Christian asked with a shrug. "How it's less than a week away? Of course not. But if we're going to try this 'having a future in long distance' thing, then can't I show some interest?"

Noah brightened. "Of course! I'm actually really excited about it. It's very open-ended. I can do almost any project I want on the artistic works of any of a dozen places or time periods. The money's great, because it means I can afford my rent without having to wait tables. Just work on art, like I like to do."

"That's really cool," Christian said. "I admit, I don't know a lot about art. But I know a great opportunity when I hear one."

"Oh, you know plenty about art!" Noah replied. "I've heard you talking about this place all the time. You know more than anyone I've ever met about this architecture."

"I guess, but that's not art."

"Architecture is, sure."

Christian laughed. "Maybe architecture is, but this place?" He gestured grandly, waving an arm in the building's general direction. "It's not old, and no one ever heard of the guy who designed it. It's no Frank Lloyd Wright."

"You have an eye for the aesthetic, though," Noah insisted. "You could do interior design, or any number of things like that."

Christian accepted the compliment. "Yeah, I guess. The truth is I never thought about it until you started talking about it like that the other night. But I find it satisfying. One day I'll walk out of this house and know that it's not a dump anymore. If I drive by it someday, then I'll know I'm the reason it's not a dump."

Noah giggled. "It's all you."

"About the grant, though, tell me more." Christian hoped to steer the conversation back to the Melton talk, because he liked the way Noah's eyes lit up when he got excited, and he was not disappointed.

"Well, the best part isn't even the money, it's the access." Noah straightened up in his seat. "The people on the board of the foundation are some of the best connected in the art world. This grant is the ultimate name-drop for backstage passes to the Met, the Louvre, etc. I can do whatever I want, wherever I want."

"That's really, really awesome. I'm so happy for you." He squeezed Noah a little harder, which Noah seemed to appreciate.

"And you?" Noah asked, flipping the conversation right back around in response to Christian's flip. "How much is left in this place?"

"Oh, it's coming along, but there's still a fair bit left to do." Christian ticked off a few items on the list in his head, all stuff he was sure Noah knew already, but his lover waited patiently and listened attentively, which made him feel appreciated.

"Most of all it's that pool." He gave a wistful sigh.

"What about the pool? The plumbing is done, the landscaping too. It's the tiling still left, right?"

"Right. The Cunninghams want me to have the original mosaic restored as much as possible."

Noah nodded. "Makes sense. From what's left, and that thing in the kitchen, it looks like it was probably very pretty when it was first installed. What's the problem?"

"You, you're the problem," he said. Christian poked Noah in the ribs, making Noah squeal in both surprise and at the tickling sensation.

"When you first got here, I promised I'd have it ready for you before you left Italy," he said, smiling sadly.

Noah beamed back at him and sighed. "You're sweet. But wasn't that just because you wanted to see me in a speedo?"

"Who says I don't still?" Christian replied.

"Horndog."

"Tease."

"I love you."

Christian sat bolt upright, shocked, and stared at Noah, who looked equally shocked at the three words that had escaped his lips.

"I... I didn't mean—"

"You didn't mean it?"

"No!" Noah shouted, waving his hands, "I mean, yes! I mean, yes I meant it, I just didn't mean to say it!"

"But…." Christian's mind was reeling. "But you did say it!"

Noah pursed his lips, and when he spoke, his voice was dripping sarcasm. "Honestly, even though I didn't plan on saying it, this isn't the reaction I would have hoped for."

"Yes!" Christian cried. "Yes, I love you too!"

He leaned forward and locked his lips onto Noah's with a passionate kiss, his arms folding around the other in an embrace, both gestures that were enthusiastically returned. The kiss was long and wonderful, and eventually led them to take things indoors.

CHAPTER 17

OF COURSE, as they knew it would, the final day came.

Noah sent his last report to the Cunninghams, going so far as to make another video call in case there were any loose ends. He was pleased to learn that there weren't any, and Mr. Cunningham told him that both he and his wife were thrilled with how hard he had worked.

"Mrs. Cunningham asked me to pass along her gratitude," he had said. "From both of us, of course."

"Of course, sir, and thank you for the opportunity. All the opportunities!"

Mr. Cunningham received his reference to the Melton grant with a benevolent smile and an incline of the head.

All of his bags were packed except for his small carry-on. He'd deal with that in the morning. He had his passport, plane tickets, everything squared away. Christian had to be at the villa in order to work with the tile expert, but he'd arranged for one of the workmen to get Noah to the airport. All that was left was a final meal together.

He made pasta the way Silvio Caravelli had taught him, which Christian noticed and complimented. The meal was quiet otherwise, neither man ignorant of what had to be filling up the other one's mind. Noah drank water instead of wine, wanting a clear head for his trip the next day and not wanting to risk allowing himself an extra glass because of his feelings. When it was finished, Christian brought up dessert.

"I didn't plan, like, a big cake or something," he said, standing and taking Noah's hand. "But I did put a little something special together."

Noah couldn't begin to guess what he meant but raised an eyebrow suggestively. "Oh?"

Christian led Noah to the bedroom they had come to share and drew from his pocket a long black cloth. He smiled and tied it around Noah's head, blindfolding him and blocking his vision almost entirely. Noah smiled also and allowed himself to be cut off from the world.

He heard Christian open the bedroom door and felt his hand being tugged lightly forward. He followed, stepping carefully just in case, for about six paces into what he believed was the center of the room. Though blindfolded he guessed that the lights were off. There was some kind of a light source in front of him, but what little light he could discern was less than there had been in the kitchen. He stopped when he felt Christian's hand on his chest.

Noah felt Christian lean closer to him and then heard a whisper in his right ear. "There's a chair to your left. I'm going to put your hand on it, and then you can sit down."

The blindfold, the sexy whispering, the feeling of Christian's warm breath on his ear, it was so stimulating that Noah felt his nipples get hard right then and there. The hairs on the back of his neck stood on end. Still unable to see, he moved slowly as Christian guided him down into what felt like the wooden chair that usually sat at the room's small computer desk. He heard movement a little ways in front of him, thought he saw a change in the lighting but couldn't be sure, then nothing.

"You can take off the blindfold now." The voice came from behind him. Noah smiled and did so. Once he could see what sat before him, that smile broadened into a grin.

Christian had shut off all the lights but one, a single light that shone down on the small wooden table in front of him. On the table was a tray, and on the tray were six glasses of wine. They alternated between red and white, three of each. The french doors and the door to the bathroom were shut, the curtains drawn so that Noah might have no extra advantage at all.

"If you're going back to New York, I thought I'd help you study."

Noah had to laugh. "I... I appreciate the thought, but I'm nowhere near ready. Seriously."

"I think you'll be pretty good at these," Christian whispered.

"Okay...." Noah reached out and picked up the first glass, about half full of a serious garnet-colored red. He took a light sniff, swirled it around in front of him for a moment, noting how its legs left trails on the glass, then gave another, deeper smell. It was very familiar somehow. He took a taste, swilled it around a bit, and swallowed.

"Medium body, good tannins," he began. "Intense, fruity flavors. I'm getting... strawberry and black cherry. Winy taste to it, little bit of wood flavor. I swear I know this wine. Have we had this before?"

His examiner said nothing.

He took another taste. "Definitely a Chianti, probably a Sangiovese.... I'm going to say the Fantini Sangiovese, recent. 2018. Am I close?"

Noah heard the rustle of movement behind him, but he didn't turn around. Christian had clearly put both work and thought into this, and he didn't want to spoil whatever was going on.

"Fantini Sangiovese," came the whisper from behind. "Familiar?"

Of course! It hit Noah like a lightning bolt, and he not only grinned all over again, but he blushed.

"Pairs well with chicken cacciatore," he said. "Like our first dinner together!"

The rustling stopped, and something big and white sailed past Noah's head. It flew into the darkness, well above the tray and the wineglasses, landing on what he assumed was Christian's bed.

The object was Christian's shirt.

"Good guess," Christian said. "Keep going."

The outline of Christian's game suddenly apparent to him, Noah eagerly picked up the next glass.

He wasn't sure how Christian had done it, but indeed he had. He'd apparently been paying close attention the entire time. Noah sampled a dry white Cabernet from the same bottling as the one they'd shared over spaghetti carbonara the first night they'd been flirting with each other and neither had really caught on. There was the red Barolo from the first time they'd really opened up about their futures over a pair of ribeye steaks, another young Chianti from the time they'd shared sandwiches and Christian had consoled him over the loss of his bedroom by inviting Noah into his own.

He also correctly identified the 2012 Vermentino from Sardinia that he'd served the night Silvio Caravelli had joined them both for dinner, and finally he came to the last glass.

"I have a wild guess," he said.

"I sure hope so," Christian replied.

While Noah had been guessing, Christian had kept up his end of the bargain. Noah had heard work boots clunk as they hit the floor and seen socks cast off into the distance one after the other. A belt had audibly clattered next to the boots, and as he went for the final glass, Noah could picture Christian, behind him in the darkness, clad only in those denim cutoffs of his. A little more worn, a little more paint-splattered than they had been when the two had first met, they fit him better than anything else he owned, and Noah had never complained about the view.

He lifted the final glass, smelled, swirled, smelled again, and tasted. As he smacked his lips a few times, he knew he was right.

"Last but not least, a definite favorite," he said. He was a little tipsy from so many glasses, but rather than slurred words, his voice had a pleasant, dreamy quality to it. "One of the top wines in Tuscany, in fact the only white wine from this region to achieve the highest Italian honors. Luminous yellow, like straw, the bouquet is delicate and aromatic. Just as much fun to smell as to drink, or almost. Pears, honeysuckle... definitely citrus. A bit heavy on the lemon, in fact, so I know it's the 2018. Some almond at the back there."

"Showoff."

Noah smiled. "It's the Vernaccia di San Gimignano, the one I served the night... the night I... that we first...."

He stammered over the words, not from intoxication at the mere tasting of wine but from how incredibly romantic he found it all. Christian finished for him.

"The night we first made love."

Noah nodded.

And then he heard the unmistakable sound of Christian undoing the buttons on the fly of the cutoffs. It was followed by the cutoffs themselves, falling to the ground at the corner of his vision. A moment later, he felt the heat of Christian behind him, beside him. He felt that strong, warm hand on his shoulder.

"Do you want to turn around?"

With all his heart, Noah did.

He turned his head, looking over his shoulder, and right at his eye level was Christian's great big beautiful penis, still shrouded by his foreskin. Noah set right to work at fixing that. Still in the chair he kissed it, then took the whole of Christian's member into his mouth and began to suck.

Christian stepped slightly back, but Noah wasn't giving up that easily. With one hand wrapped around the shaft and the other cradling Christian's big, heavy balls, Noah teased and licked at the foreskin in hopes of getting that purple head to come out sooner. It quickly became apparent, however, that Christian was not backing away from him but actually stepping around and in front of Noah. It was awkward, but Noah did not relinquish his hold on that cock he'd come to know so intimately in their time together. Christian straddled Noah on the chair, and Noah took to his pleasures in earnest.

He alternated between playful licks like a lollipop and deep dives in an effort to fill his mouth with that wonderful cock, hoping to bring Christian to a full erection as soon as possible. He didn't have long to wait. After less than a minute of fondling, caressing, and sucking, he felt the foreskin slowly retracting under the ministrations of his tongue, and the soft skin of the head was pressing against the roof of his mouth like an erotic offering. He pulled it out so he could see it, slick with his saliva and glistening in the remaining light over the wine tray, and the sight filled him with joy and hunger like he had never known.

As he went back down, slowly urging that monster dick farther and farther down his throat, he noticed that his lover was not idle. Christian ran his fingers through Noah's blond hair, grown longer since he'd arrived in Italy without regular access to his stylist, long enough for Christian to pull on. After their first encounter, they'd discovered that while Christian was only mildly aroused by such stimulation, Noah loved it. The passing thought went through Noah's head that in Christian, he had someone who had learned his likes and dislikes, as he had Christian's, and whether he wanted to risk never finding that again.

But then Christian was pulling his hair, eliciting moans of pleasure from Noah despite the fat cock around which he'd wrapped his lips, and all worry or concern for the future was cast aside.

Next to be cast aside was Noah's shirt, Christian pulling it up and over his head, which resulted in a moment of Noah having to stop working the dick, but only for a moment. Once the shirt was off Christian was able to play not only with Noah's hair but also his nipples, and Noah went wild.

He pushed all the way down, feeling the tender head of Christian's cock against the back of his throat and the tickle of Christian's pubic hair against his nose. The smell was overwhelming, the scent of Christian and just raw manhood, and for the briefest moment before he pulled it out again, he felt Christian's hanging balls brush against his chin. It was pure ecstasy.

Between the dick in his mouth, the hand running through his hair, and the other hand brushing, stroking, and tweaking his nipples Noah was beginning to get uncomfortable... inside his own shorts, that is. His penis yearned for release, at full extension like he'd never known before, hard and hammering in his crotch and needing to be free.

He tapped Christian on the abdomen, and his lover dutifully pulled out. Noah looked up to see that warm, smiling face, backlit by whatever light he'd set up for the wine test.

"I need to get out of these clothes," he said.

Christian grinned and agreed.

The next thing he knew he was up in the air. Christian, whose muscles even Noah had apparently underestimated, hoisted him up in both arms. Noah felt like a koala bear in the man's hug and laughed at the idea. The feeling of his lover's penis, warm and hard as steel, as it pressed against the bare skin of his thigh was tantalizing when Noah pictured all the things it would soon be used for. Christian spun him around and half placed, half flung him onto the bed.

It occurred to Noah that now they were away from the light, his eyes were starting to adjust to the darkness. The scant moonlight that made it past the curtains on the french doors was enough for him to make out first the outline of Christian's chiseled form, and soon enough the features.

Noah lay back on the bed as Christian fumbled in the darkness at his crotch. He heard his belt come loose, then his fly, followed by shorts and boxers tugged down to his knees and over his feet so quickly that he barely had time to lift his ass off the bed. Christian let loose another hungry growl, involuntary and almost feral, the mere sound of which sent ripples down Noah's body and terminated at the point of his cock.

He could tell Christian was about to go down on him, giving lover that he was in search of returning a favor, but Noah pulled at his shoulders. The bigger man allowed himself to be drawn onto the bed, his own erection still engorged and leaking fluids, and Noah flipped around to suckle at it once more. Taking the cue, Christian pursed his own lips to allow Noah's penis to press gently through their saliva-coated opening so he could do the same. A slow, rapturous sixty-nine began.

Noah was uncertain which he enjoyed more: the delicious, wet, pounding muscle of Christian's cock in his mouth or the warm, soft, enveloping feeling of Christian's mouth around his own. In the time they'd been together, Christian had learned all his ins and outs, literally, and Noah could feel him putting his knowledge to use. As the fingers wrapped around his balls gently moved further, one beginning to poke and lightly stroke at his asshole, he found himself smiling even as he bobbed up and down on Christian's dick.

He released Christian from between his lips and looked down, the erection throbbing and raging, simply dripping with saliva from Noah's care, and then he looked farther down at Christian. When he caught the other man's eye, Noah merely nodded to indicate that he was ready for more. Christian, all hard muscle on the outside in contrast to the soft, sweet man that Noah had come to know, grinned a dopey idiot grin with Noah's pale dick still in his mouth. Noah was briefly taken aback by the appearance of his own cock. The feathery bush of pubic hair was as he remembered it but the long white shaft and pink head were so hard and ready that his organ looked bigger than he thought he'd ever seen it before.

With lust and with longing, he pictured the eventual orgasm that thing would bring.

"How do you want it?" Noah asked. He was prepared to get down on all fours, his face smashed into those comfortable pillows as Christian smashed into him, but he had a suspicion he already knew. His lover liked to see the pleasure written on his face.

Christian arose from his loving strokes to kneel on the bed facing Noah, naked and erect, the only strong light in the room being the light coming shining onto his face and chest, and Noah was struck with the idea that it was like a very god was kneeling before him. The art historian in him compared what he saw to paintings from Michelangelo or Caravaggio, an Adonis gazing down at him in his nakedness.

When Adonis leaned down and kissed him, Noah was not prepared. Their juices mingled as their tongues did, Noah could taste his own sweetness still on Christian's breath, and he hoped Christian could taste the same.

"On your back," Adonis said. "I want to see those baby blues while I pound."

It was so ridiculous, the picture of a masculine god talking like they were at a New York bathhouse, Noah had to laugh. Christian only smiled, his face betraying joy that Noah had gotten the joke but the rest of his body undeterred. Noah turned around until his head was on the pillow and his legs on Christian's shoulders. Applying some of their mingled saliva into the crack of Noah's ass, Christian began to ease forward. Noah bit his lip, arched his back, and waited for the bliss he had come to know so well.

Sliding into him, slowly but surely, Noah felt every inch of Christian pressing forward into his hole and couldn't hold back a little moue of pleasure. As he felt himself widen, filled to the brim until he could stand no more, he felt the light tickle of Christian's pubic hair around his sphincter and the dam was burst: he cried aloud with joy.

Christian smiled down at him, began to withdraw, and then to enter once more. The long, slow strokes were tender, as if Christian were savoring the sensation. Noah was only going to let him get away with that for so long.

He took both of Christian's hands away from his hips and pulled his lover down to meet his gaze. Christian, never fully pulling out, took the opportunity to kiss Noah again, which Noah enjoyed, but when the kiss was done, he stared hard into Christian's eyes and made his true intentions clear.

"Fuck me like you mean it," he hissed.

If Christian was surprised at Noah's directness, he recovered quickly. "Yes, sir," he replied, and began to thrust again.

Before long he was moving in and out, in and out, a piston of manhood pumping away at Noah's hole and driving Noah's squealing into screams. Christian's hands ran up and down the sides of his body, from squeezing his buttocks up past his hips and along his rib cage to his armpits, where they would turn around and go back. As he felt every part of his body being stroked this way, inside and out, Noah spread his arms wide and grabbed pillows on either side of him as he gloried in being simply taken, taken in animal lust.

Christian's cock, an extension of his lustful fury, pounded in and out over and over, each time slamming that secret place inside him that meant pleasures untold, and Noah could not restrain himself to be quiet as his lover did so.

It did not escape Noah's notice that, far from being lost in the grips of his own delight as their passion passed between them, Christian eventually reached down to grasp Noah's own penis, his firm hand intent on keeping it erect and bringing it to a climax of its own. Noah allowed himself to be pulled and tugged at one end, even while being pushed and thrusted at the other, enjoying every minute of their wild lovemaking.

When Christian began picking up speed, however, and his grip around Noah's cock tightened as it stroked, Noah knew his partner well enough to know what was coming. He welcomed it with every fiber of his being.

"Yes, yes, yes!" he screamed, thrashing his head back and forth on the pillow, squeezing the muscles of his derriere tight around the penetrating organ of this man, this wonderful man who he had come to know, to rely on, to love.

Christian too seemed unable to restrain himself, with grunts of effort and thrill issuing forth from his throat with every pound and push.

It was in a moment of perfect oneness, two bodies so entangled with each other that their souls might so entangle as well, that both men came with urgent, shuddering pleasure.

Noah felt the frictionate thrusting come to an end, and a deliriously beautiful pumping was begun. He felt Christian, all of Christian, flow into the darkest places of him, as if shining a light from which he hoped he would never falter. In the same moment, he achieved his own finish, Christian's loving hand never releasing his rampant cock, and he burst load after load of his most vital essence in a fountainous display. As some arrived on his forehead, which was sweaty from the workout, he pictured it like a Vegas fountain to which Christian had turned on the lights. He concentrated on the feeling of Christian spending the last of himself inside him, urgently pushing out a few more thrusts as if he hoped the climactic moment would never end.

CHRISTIAN LEANED down for another kiss and was more than glad that Noah reciprocated, deeply. Their tongues twirled as they soothed each other through the final tremors and into the afterglow. Pulling himself out of this man he had come to love, Christian turned on one side and lay next to him.

For a long time they simply looked at each other, each panting for breath and drinking in the sight of the other man as they might drink and pant at a desert oasis. Betraying the softer side of him that he had never known he had, not until Noah brought it out of him, Christian felt a single tear roll down his cheek.

"Don't," Noah said.

"Sorry."

"I know."

They kissed once more, and Noah curled up in Christian's embrace. He was soon asleep, but Christian didn't drift off until much, much later. He cursed his cowardice for not saying he would go to New York with Noah when it had come up. Who knew what could've happened? It might not have been as bad as all that. In his darkest moments, against his will and shocked at himself immediately after doing so, he also cursed Noah for starting something under that roof which would likely never be finished. It was disingenuous of him at best, but he couldn't help it. The potential pitfalls of an ongoing long-distance relationship were many. Even if they maintained their connection, when would they see each other again?

He stayed awake longer than he meant to, holding Noah close longer than he meant to, dreading the next night at the villa. The night when he would once again be alone.

CHAPTER 18

A WEEK later Noah's entire world was back where it had begun, with a few variations. He was back at the cafe in New York City waiting tables for what he hoped would be the last time ever. At home, of course, only an internet connection away, was the variation that brought a smile to his face against even the harshest of customer complaints.

In his uniform outfit of black pants, white dress shirt, black tie, and apron, he walked over to a table under an umbrella in the sun and bent down to smile at the older woman and her dog, who he'd been dutifully supplying with hot water for tea for almost an hour. He spoke up when addressing her.

"How're you doing over here, Mrs. Merrihew? Anything I can get you? More hot water? Something for Agnes?"

"Oh no, we're fine," she said merrily, holding up Agnes's little paw to wave at Noah for the umpteenth time. "Just two old ladies, out on the town!"

He knocked his professional smile up from a four to a six and gave a polite nod. "You just let me know of anything, okay?" She nodded in reply.

Noah turned around on his heel, a little quicker than he'd meant to, but his speed meant he was fast enough to catch one of the men at a nearby table staring at him. The man wore a dark suit and a crisp blue tie, his hair slicked back with the perfect amount of mousse, and he was holding a coffee cup. He hurriedly looked at his lunch companions, who were chatting away, before realizing he'd been caught. He looked back at Noah, smiled, tilted both eyebrows up and down just once, then toasted with his coffee mug.

Noah smiled politely back, more of a three than a real smile, and walked over. "Did you need more coffee? I know I'm not your regular server, but if you need more coffee, I can get that."

"No," he said, taking a sip and looking Noah up and down. "I think I've got everything I need."

"Glad to hear it," Noah said, smiling a one and heading back into the cafe's kitchen. He resolved a few orders, answered questions about Tuscany, and yes, he said, he certainly was excited to be quitting and working on art full-time. The boss wasn't talking to him, and Noah understood. He had taken Noah back after two months away, when he easily could've replaced him with one of New York City's million other waiters, only to find out it was temporary. The Melton grant committee was going to hear his proposal in just a few days, and then the checks would start rolling in.

If I ever settle on a proposal, that is, Noah rebuked himself.

By the time he found his way back to Mrs. Merrihew and checked on her once more, the Wall Street guys had paid and left.

"Now I know it's none of my business," Mrs. Merrihew said in that voice people use when they're going to say something anyway and don't want to have to apologize. "But I saw the way that young man was looking at you. You shut that fella down a little hard, y'know."

Noah smiled at her, a genuine smile not born of customer service or the desire for a tip. She was a regular at the cafe, and Noah liked her. "Mrs. M, I'm working. I shouldn't have to put up with that at work."

"Oh, of course not," she readily agreed. "But a nice young man like you in New York City? Would it hurt to get a phone number?"

Noah chuckled and knelt down next to her table in order to scratch Agnes around the ears. The little white terrier was happy for the attention.

"I appreciate the concern, Mrs. M, but I'm spoken for," he said, leaning one arm on the table to look back up at the older woman.

She raised an eyebrow. "Oh? What is he, then, some kind of longshoreman? Navy? Does he work on an offshore oil rig?"

"What a colorfully maritime imagination you have, Mrs. M."

Mrs. Merrihew tutted at him. "Respect your elders. What I mean is that you say you have someone, but I can sense a boy who's not been touched in far too long at fifty paces."

Noah bristled. "Mrs. M, you're a great lady and I do respect you, but if I don't have to put up with intrusions into my romantic life from finance guys while I'm working, then I don't need accusations from you either."

"I'm sorry," she sighed. "You're right, that was forward of me. She took his chin in her hand, her skin papery but warm, and looked in his eyes. "You just look... sad, somehow."

"I guess." Noah scratched the dog some more. "He's... it's complicated. Long distance."

"Called it." The old woman nodded. She let go of him and sipped her tea. "I understand. Well, that's a shame. I hope you come to your senses. Or he does."

"I think I know where my senses are, Mrs. M."

"Not if you're here and he isn't," she said. She gave a laugh too, half snort and half cackle. "Or at least one of you doesn't."

Noah stood up, and by the time he'd smoothed his apron, he had his customer-service smile back on. "You're sweet to think of me, Mrs. M. Anything else I can get you?"

"No, we'd better be going. Agnes and I have an appointment with the dog groomer, and then my gigolo."

"Okay, Mrs. M."

Noah knew better than to touch that one with a ten-foot pole. She was either setting up a joke or being painfully truthful and neither was more likely than the other, so it was best to just move on.

At the end of his shift he hung up his apron for the last time, gave a few kisses and goodbye hugs, and headed back home. He'd sublet his apartment to a friend from the school, a decent guy named Brendan who was originally from London but doing a summer in New York City. They hadn't known each other well, but enough friends had vouched for him that Noah wasn't worried about him wrecking the place, and indeed he had not. When Noah left it had seemed like the perfect solution. There wasn't supposed to be any overlap between the dates of either of them coming or going so that would be that.

Instead Noah had returned to find that his friend's program had been extended another month. Noah hadn't planned on living in his tiny one-bedroom with a roommate, but if he stuck to the terms of the original agreement, he'd be throwing Brendan out into the street. Unwilling to let that happen to someone who'd gotten him out of a jam for two months and seemed to be a decent guy, Noah had agreed to share the place for a month.

Unfortunately, he quickly discovered that their personalities and lifestyles could not be more opposite. Where Noah was neat, Brendan was a slob. Where Noah was punctual, Brendan was out till all hours every night. When he got home, he dashed into the bedroom, eager to get onto the internet and visit with Christian before Brendan got home and started making noise.

"Hey, babe!" he shouted at his laptop when the screen popped up. Across the ocean, in a familiar little villa in Tuscany, the camera was zoomed close on Christian's smiling face.

"Hey to you too! Aww, you didn't need to dress up just for me."

Noah looked down and laughed, he hadn't even realized he was still dressed for work. "Oh, this old thing? Well, y'know."

Christian laughed too, and the sound washed away all the minor annoyances that had crossed Noah's day.

"I just got home from work. You don't mind if I change while we chat, do you?"

"Are you kidding? It's the highlight of my day."

"Horndog."

"Hottie."

Noah smiled and began to unbutton his white dress shirt. On the other end he watched the view jiggle and shake as Christian too became more comfortable. It didn't escape his notice that Christian was dressed in his work outfit too: those paint-stained cutoff jeans that he remembered so well. From the backdrop, he was clearly sitting in his bed in the large guest bedroom, and he looked very comfortable.

Seeing him like that was like a stabbing pain in Noah's chest, but he said nothing.

"How's the house coming?" he asked instead.

As if sensing that Noah was interested but also wanted to fill the silence, Christian started to talk. He filled Noah in on the progress of the pool, the work of the tiling guys who had finally been contracted, and a lot of the other little things.

"Your office is getting torn up too, at last," he said.

Noah discarded his work pants and socks and plopped down onto his mattress in his boxers. "My office? You mean that second guest room?"

Christian shook his head. "No, your real office. The wine cellar. The electrician is back, fixing up the lighting, and I got a guy who's going to set up a separate heating and cooling unit down there. It's not the same as rezoning the entire HVAC system, but that'd mean tearing apart the house again when I just got it all fixed."

"That's great news. Do you still have all the specs I gave you on how to take care of the wine?"

"Yes, dear," Christian said, rolling his eyes as he put sarcastic emphasis on the last word.

Noah smiled, but his eyes began to well up with tears.

"Hey," Christian said, noticing. "I'm sorry. I didn't mean it like that."

"No, I'm not mad or anything. Just... you just sounded really familiar right then, and it made me miss you even harder for a moment."

Christian looked away.

"Sorry," Noah said. He wiped his eyes. "I didn't mean to bring the moment down. It's just so good to talk to you again."

When Christian looked back, he was smiling. "How's the grant stuff going?" he asked. He was trying to change the subject, and Noah appreciated it.

"Oh, y'know, it's crazy. I have to write up this proposal and give this whole demonstration. They want to read a prospectus that I don't really have time to write. Leaving the cafe was just the first step. I have to get out into the art world and see museums, talk to curators, a whole lot of work in not a lot of time."

"And the cafe? Mrs. M still a good tipper?"

"To the very end," Noah said with a laugh. "We should introduce her to your grandfather if we ever get the chance. They'd get along great."

"I bet. Y'know, there are a lot of great art museums in Florence, just a short drive from here. If any of them were, I don't know, good enough for you to study. No pressure, just a thought I had while I was working today."

Noah paused. The truth was that he had considered it, actually. Florence just didn't have what he needed, though, and he wasn't sure how to explain that to Christian. The art of the Italian renaissance painters, of which Florence had an abundant supply, had been written about over and over. The subject had been done to death. He couldn't think of anything innovative or interesting to say or do in Florence, and he didn't know how to break that news to the man he'd fallen in love with.

There was one idea forming at the back of his mind that was worthy of more consideration, but he didn't want to get Christian's hopes up, so he didn't say anything about it yet.

He admitted that Florence was a great art city and then talked more about the trials and tribulations of his day as a food service worker. Christian was both attentive and supportive, a combination which bolstered Noah and also sometimes broke his heart. After an hour of chatting, Noah looked at the clock on his dresser that he kept on "Christian time."

"Oh my god, babe, it's almost midnight where you are!"

Christian shrugged. "What can I say, I'm a sucker for good company."

Noah heard the sounds of movement on the other side of his bedroom door. At the very least Brendan was home, and it even sounded like he might've brought friends. If he knew Christian, and he did, the boy would keep talking with him into the wee hours and ruin his own following day if given half a chance. Brendan's arrival was as good an excuse as any to end the conversation for Christian's own good.

"I should get going," he said. "Roommate's here."

"Sure, totally," Christian replied. Noah wasn't sure if he was imagining the hint of sadness in his voice but figured he probably wasn't. "Same time tomorrow?"

Noah smiled. "Tomorrow and every day after that."

Then it was Christian's turn to smile. "Until I see you again."

"The best day."

They ended the call, and Noah allowed himself to stare at the screen for a little bit longer. Then he pulled on a T-shirt and some shorts and went out into the apartment.

As evinced immediately by the loud music and chatter of people, Brendan wasn't alone. It wasn't as bad as he'd feared. He'd been afraid his unintentional roommate had brought home a party or something, but it turned out to just be three especially loud and rambunctious friends who wanted everyone in the borough to hear their other friend's new album. There were wineglasses out already but, Noah noted gratefully, no cigarette butts.

"Brendan," he shouted at his roommate, "can you just turn it down a little?"

"Oh, sorry, love," the Brit said, and immediately jumped out of the sofa (which doubled as Brendan's bed) and did so. Brendan wasn't a jerk, they just weren't a good fit. Noah thanked him and headed into the kitchenette for something to eat.

One of the guests also got up off the couch and followed him. Despite the long day he'd had, despite the video chat with Christian still at the forefront of his mind, Noah couldn't help but admire the attractive stranger. Earlier in the day it had been easy to ignore the attentions of Mr. Wall Street (he'd been working for goodness' sake, and that wasn't his type anyway), but the newcomer was a different drink of water all together. He was tall and skinny, lanky almost, with dirty-blond hair that reached down to his shoulders in shaggy locks and what looked like a permanently goofy smile. He wore a black

T-shirt with no sleeves and the name of a band that Noah had never heard of, with tight blue jeans and sneakers.

"I hope you don't mind," he said with a slight British accent, "but we broke into your wine."

"Oh," Noah said. "Sure, that's no big deal. Brendan knows it's there to share."

The goofy smile materialized into a childish grin, and Noah smiled back despite himself. He pulled a carryout meal from the cafe out of the fridge and went searching for a fork. When he found one he stopped, pulling a permanent marker out of the kitchen drawer also so he could write his name on the outside just in case he didn't finish. The lanky man laughed.

"Good idea, mate," the Brit said. "Brendan'll eat anything."

"Don't I know it."

The lanky man leaned against the kitchen counter, still looking at Noah and smiling but slightly blocking his path, and offered a hand to shake. "I'm Blake. You're Noah, right?"

It suddenly dawned on Noah just what was happening here. He looked out through the pass-through from the kitchen to the living room proper and saw that Brendan was very obviously not looking in his direction. Pointedly, in fact, he was looking almost anywhere else as he chatted about the music with a pale girl with black-and-purple dreadlocks.

Brendan, who Noah recalled had expressed that he didn't believe in long-distance relationships. This was a setup. It was time to shut Blake down, politely but firmly.

He did shake the offered hand. "Yup, that's me. Nice meeting you."

Noah tried to push past Blake and exit the kitchen. Blake didn't stop him physically, but his body language made it clear he wasn't giving up that easily.

"Brendan says you just got back from two months in Italy? I've been to Florence, on vacation with my parents once. Did you get to see a lot of the museums?"

Not wanting to be rude, Noah stopped at the doorway and looked back in. "I didn't, actually. My only time in Florence was from traveling through. I was in Italy for work."

Blake nodded, taking a sip off his wineglass. "Sounds interesting. Work... with wine, yeah?"

"Yup," Noah affirmed. "Look, I don't want to be rude, but I'm really tired and I just got off my last shift at work so... it was nice to meet you, but I'm going to hit the hay."

"Oh, for sure," Blake said. "Sorry, I didn't mean to hold you up. Last day of work, though? We're all going to this party tomorrow. You should come with us and we'll celebrate!"

Noah, who had been about to turn and start walking away, finally put on his customer-service smile. "Appreciated. I'll think about it."

Blake smiled and ran his fingers through his own hair, lifting his shirt as he did so and exposing not just an armpit but a nipple as well. Noah knew when he was being flirted with, and in a moment that felt like betrayal, he kind of enjoyed it.

"Night!" he said.

"Night," Blake replied, smiling again over another sip of wine.

"Sorry about stealing your vee-no, mate," Brendan said as Noah walked through the living room. "Didn't think it would be a problem, what with you always going on about how you love to share it."

"No, of course, it's no problem," Noah said. He was consciously pushing his mind back onto Christian when he stopped.

Sitting on its side on the coffee table, empty to the last drop, was a bottle of Vernaccia di San Gimignano that Noah had brought back through customs.

He sighed.

"No problem at all. I'm going to bed."

"Bed?" Brendan asked, a half-smile on his lips. "It's Saturday night and the night's still young!"

"Yeah, I'm going to bed, Brendan!" he said, sharper than he meant to. He'd had his fill for one day of coworkers, customers, and now roommates who seemed to think that his relationship with Christian was flexible because it was long distance.

The group stopped chatting and stared at him.

"Sorry." Noah waved apologetically. "I'm, uh, I'm still on Italy time."

Brendan smiled and laughed, an attempt at playing off solidarity with a fellow world traveler, and went back to his guests. Blake continued to watch as Noah went to his bedroom, where he shut the door and sat on the bed to eat his dinner.

He thought about calling Christian again. He thought about how everything would feel all right again if he had Christian's arms around him, and about how nothing had been right since he'd come home. For just a moment he fooled himself into thinking Christian was there, that he'd be right there if Noah just rolled over in the bed. Of course, he wasn't.

By the time he was done eating, he knew that the time difference was the real reason not to. They had acknowledged it was almost midnight, and by now it was even later. Christian needed his sleep. He had no doubt that Christian would joyfully wake up and talk to him if he wanted him to, but Noah didn't want to be that guy. Not wanting to risk another interaction with Blake, he sealed the leftovers and placed them by the door, where they'd keep at least until the next morning. Noah curled into bed, content that he wasn't keeping his boyfriend up late with no reason.

Well, Noah thought with a smile as he drifted off to sleep. *Not without me there, there isn't.*

He cuddled his body pillow for a while until it was nice and warm, then spontaneously got out of bed, undressed completely, and crawled back between the covers with the pillow at his back. The noise from the living room wasn't too bad, so he worked on falling asleep. He wondered why he was no longer comfortable wearing a T-shirt and boxers to bed. It certainly made more sense in New York, with the different climate, and even more so with a roommate who wasn't also his romantic partner.

Deciding that it didn't matter, he drew close to the big, warm body pillow situated behind him and was soon fast asleep. He dreamed that it was someone else big and warm behind him but awoke disappointed.

Noah awoke the next morning to the early morning sun pouring in his window, the smell of coffee brewing in the kitchen's automatic pot, and the sound of snoring coming from the living room. His first thought was to wonder whether Brendan had brought some sort of a bull into the apartment, but he rapidly deduced that it was a sound enhanced by the virtue of being multiple sounds rolled into one. The evening guests had become sleepover guests, it seemed. He pulled on some sleep pants and a T-shirt and bravely stepped out into his own apartment.

The smell, he was grateful to discern, wasn't that bad. Brendan was curled up in an uncomfortable-looking tangle with the girl with the dreadlocks, and someone who could only be Blake was lying facedown on the love seat, his ankles dangling off the far end, his head turned away from Noah. The face wasn't visible, but the hair was unmistakable.

Also unmistakable was Blake's state of dress… or undress, rather. He wore nothing but a pair of tight white briefs, immaculately clean Noah was pleased to discover, briefs that showed off the shape and curves of Blake's ass in a most delightful way.

Noah heard a voice at the back of his mind, a prurient voice of which he was not proud, purring as it expressed approval of Blake in his underwear. Noah's better angels shouted the voice down, and he went for coffee.

As he poured, fixed, and drank the coffee, he considered his day. The Cunninghams had left a few emails with last-minute questions of clarification that he felt obligated to answer, and then there was the Melton grant. It was guaranteed to him—he might have seriously considered staying in Tuscany if it hadn't been—but he had to put together his proposal for how to use it. The idea pulling at the corners of his brain pulled a little harder. He had interviews scheduled with some curators at small art museums in the city in hopes that the power of the grant might get him into their private collections so he could create a truly impressive presentation for the board.

Noah heard rustling coming from the living room and figured Brendan was waking up. A light sleeper at the best of times, he'd no doubt smelled the coffee and was ready to begin the day. The little devil voice at the back of Noah's mind wondered whether Blake was up too, and Noah squashed it down again.

He stepped out into the living room and saw that while Brendan was still fast asleep, Blake was indeed up... in one sense of the word, anyway. He had rolled over onto his back, one arm draped over his eyes, and the first thing Noah noticed was a tattoo on Blake's side, just to the right of his abdomen, which said "Carpe Diem" in scrollwork letters that were encircled with a thorny vine. Just below that, the second thing Noah noticed was Blake's erection.

That little devil voice at the back of Noah's mind offered another opinion. And then a suggestion.

Noah couldn't help himself. He took in the sight of the nearly naked man stretched out in his living room. Based on personal experience, he guessed that dick had to be at least eight inches long and wide around... a thing of beauty, he had no doubt.

Immediately he felt guilty and then conflicted. *I'm allowed to look at other guys*, he thought to himself. *As long as it's just looking. Christian and I never discussed "rules" or anything. I can look... maybe think about it a little.*

As a compromise to the little devil voice he agreed that looking wasn't cheating, but looking lustfully at someone when they were nearly naked and wholly unconscious was unacceptable both in and out of a relationship. He shook himself and turned to walk away.

Then he saw that just below the arm draped over his eyes, Blake was smiling. He had to be awake. Flustered, Noah looked away and went back to the bedroom. Minutes later he was on the computer and Christian was answering his call.

"What's up, Noah?"

"Am I interrupting you?"

"Naw, I was having lunch. Is everything okay?"

"Yeah," Noah said, sipping his coffee. "I… I just wanted to hear your voice."

CHAPTER 19

SMILING, CHRISTIAN closed his laptop at the end of the call. It was older and more weathered than Noah's, barely equal to the task of video chats when you came right down to it, but it did the job. He put the thing on the bedside table.

Something had seemed to be bothering Noah when he'd called, something Christian couldn't quite put his finger on. By the end of it he seemed to be feeling better, though, and like the good boyfriend he was, Christian was happy just to have helped.

He leaned back and looked out the window. That sun was bright and strong, shining down into his bedroom through the french doors, turning up the heat throughout the entire house. The day was at its hottest point and showed no signs of stopping. He got out of bed to get back to work.

The workmen were on a lunch break just like he was, but checking his watch, he noticed that he'd let it go for far too long. It was hard to justify being a harsh taskmaster with them: the house was nearly complete. The new tilework in the pool was really all that was left, and that project was well underway. There was no direct door from his guest room to the pool, so he went through Noah's room to see how things were doing.

He always walked quickly through that room. He'd had all the linens changed, and a team of cleaning ladies had been through it, but he swore he could still smell Noah there. Every time he set foot inside, he expected to see that cute smile (or that perky ass) greeting him from the bed.

The truth was that, for a long-distance relationship, things were actually going unexpectedly well. They spoke often, for which Christian was grateful, and he was happy that Noah was in a busy place surrounded by people. He sometimes found life in the somewhat isolated villa a little boring, or at least lonely. The workmen who came every day were solid fellows, but they were his contracted employees. His grandfather came up from time to time to check on things or to keep him company, but the number of people in his life had dropped from dozens of not-so-close friends in Miami to one or two people in Italy. He was glad Noah had lots of people around.

Though he didn't like to admit it, he sometimes worried over the thought that the Noah he had come to know and love was actually the exact opposite: a loner where Christian liked crowds, perfectly comfortable with just his own company. Did a personality difference like that mean they weren't meant to be?

The tiling expert was hard at work directing the crew around the pool when Christian arrived. He had complied with the man's every request, viewing it as his own opportunity to hop out of the driver's seat. The man even had a better gift for getting the remaining workmen to wrap up their lunch breaks than Christian, so he was pleased to find them well underway.

"Where do you want me?" he asked.

The expert threw up his hands with a joyful expression and began to answer Christian in rapid-fire Italian. Christian spoke the language almost fluently but not well enough to keep up. Eventually the tiling expert gathered from Christian's blank expression that he was not making himself known, and he directed Christian into the drained pool.

"Finally," he said in broken English, "the one with the hands of skills! Please to take center mosaic." He gestured to Poseidon, half-formed on the pool's bottom.

With a smile at the idea of a chance to work with his hands, a thing he'd have found ironic two months ago, Christian climbed down and went at it.

At the end of the day, he decided to walk the house while the workmen were clearing up, doing the first of what he assumed would be many spot checks. The Cunninghams weren't due for another week or more, so he had plenty of time, but he wanted everything to be just right. He inspected the guest rooms and decided all were in perfect shape. Even his own was as done as it was going to be, just needing to be turned down by the cleaning ladies on Christian's last day.

He walked through the main entrance, the few damaged tiles of which had been restored early in the process. It was definitely ready for the owners to see. He toured the study, the library, the master bedroom, all of the rooms as he left the kitchen for last. When there was no more putting it off, he took a gulp and a breath and went in.

It was immaculate, of course. The cleaning ladies had done a bang-up job, and he'd done his best to keep it that way rather than have to pay them to come in more often. He didn't expect them back until the final sweep right before the Cunninghams arrived. He had planned to go straight through to the wine cellar and check on the work there, but in the kitchen, he got caught up in memories.

He saw the stove where Noah had made him their meals. The little table where they'd eaten together every night. The door out to the patio where they sat in each other's arms and watched the stars. The kitchen counter where they'd first fucked, during a thunderstorm he recalled, their two bodies finally giving in to the ache they felt for each other.

Christian felt himself starting to cry. He loved Noah, and to his nervous surprise and constant joy Noah still loved him. But not knowing when they'd ever see each other again was tearing him apart. He shut the door to the pool and sat down at the table so none of the burly, masculine workers would see him and say something, and then he allowed himself time for tears.

After a minute or two, he heard a little cough from the kitchen door. He sat up sharply, cursing the workmen in his mind, wiping away his tears before he turned around to look. When he did it wasn't the tiling expert, ready to be snooty about the quality of hand-fired Italian mosaic tile, nor the workmen ready to call him "lover boy" and other names. It was his granddad, Silvio, his cane in one hand and leaning on the doorway with the other shoulder.

"Hey," was all Christian could think to say.

"Buongiorno," his granddad said. "Or should I say good afternoon."

"Probably afternoon, yeah."

The old man walked over to the kitchen table, pausing to put a comforting hand on Christian's shoulder before he lowered himself into an opposing chair. He looked like he had something serious he wanted to say, but at the last minute thought better of it.

"I came to discuss this thing that you want to do," he said. "This internet thing. Perhaps I am too old and I do not fully understand, but I want you to explain again."

Christian focused. "The problem is your internet presence, Granddad. You're not advertising the business well online. That's probably why the Cunningham contract is the first big one you've gotten in two years."

"Excuse me," Silvio said, sitting up straight. "But Silvio Caravelli has never wanted for work."

"No, but a lot of that work has been small. And you only got this job because you happened to live right here, and word of mouth worked in your favor."

"Perhaps."

The truth of his granddad's internet marketing skills, he knew, was even more dire than he was letting on. His granddad's "website," if it could even be called that, was a monstrosity. It looked like it had been made in 1997, and Christian feared that it probably had been, that his own father might've been the one to help Granddad set it up.

"While I'm here let me put the fancy degree my parents paid for to good use, Granddad. Let me redesign your website, get your name out there to clients—"

"Oh, knowing how to lay a tile design means you know how to design websites too?" the old man asked.

"I'm not as good as a professional," Christian admitted. "But they're a lot simpler than they used to be. I can put together a good one for real cheap."

Silvio Caravelli's eyebrow went up. Instantly Christian knew he'd used the wrong word.

"And just how much is this going to cost me?" he asked.

"I can do all of it for free," Christian told him. "While I'm in Italy I can set the whole thing up, and if I wind up back in the States, I can maintain it from there. A basic website, a social media presence, I can get it all up and running and show you how to work it from anywhere in the world."

The idea of teaching his granddad how to use Twitter caused an involuntary physical shuddering to quake through Christian's body, but Silvio didn't notice.

"'While I'm here,'" Silvio said, "'while I'm in Italy,' and 'if I wind up back in the States.' Are you planning on rushing off? Maybe...." The old man's voice softened. "Maybe to New York City?"

The younger man laughed. "Can you just see me, Granddad? Another Italian-American guy in New York City?" He exaggerated a New York accent, pronouncing it more like "Noo Yoak," and Silvio laughed.

"It is not so ridiculous," he replied, "if it's what you want."

"Nah. I've invested a lot of time and effort here, Granddad. Learning the contracts, the permitting, cleaning up my Italian."

Silvio Caravelli harrumphed at the notion that Christian's Italian had improved, but Christian kept talking before he could comment.

"What I mean is that things are going well right here in Italy. I got everything I need."

His grandfather raised one eyebrow, gently and without sarcasm. "Everything?"

Christian thought about precisely that every single day. But as much as he wanted Noah off the screen and into his arms, that just wasn't his world.

"I'm not making any decisions until the villa's done," he said. "I want it to be perfect. I know I'm young, at least that's how it feels like the Cunninghams think of me, and I want them to agree that they trusted the right person. I want to be worthy of their faith."

"My boy, nothing in this world could be more true." Silvio pounded the table, his face beaming. "You are certainly worthy of mine."

Christian blushed a little but gave a shy thank-you in reply. There was a brief silence, and he watched as his grandfather got that look again. The look of whatever serious thing he'd really come to say. But Christian already knew.

"It's today, isn't it," he said. It wasn't really a question.

The old man nodded. "I had hoped to spare you this sorrow, especially after your boy went away, but the day has come. Your father tells me the divorce will be finalized tomorrow."

Christian sighed. He'd known the day was coming. Suspected it ever since the day his dad had contacted his granddad about annulment, but he had been certain for quite some time after. He rolled the idea around in his head, thinking, nodding to himself.

"Good," he finally said.

Silvio arched a bushy, inquiring eyebrow. Christian threw up his hands.

"If them staying together for the next twenty years means twenty years of them yelling at each other, then it's good. Obviously I'd love it if they could fix it all and patch things up, but that's just going back to the way things used to be. Sometimes it's just not meant to be...."

As the significance of his own words in his own situation dawned on him, Christian's eyes grew hot once more. He looked away from his grandfather.

"My boy...," the old man began, but his voice trailed off. For all his years, all his experiences and his wisdom, he just didn't seem to know what to say.

Christian looked up suddenly. "Can I stay here with you?" He wiped the tears from his eyes. "I don't want to go back to Miami. There's nothing for me there now. What, I couch surf with whichever of them will take me while I bounce around and try to find a real job? Screw that."

"What about Noah?"

Christian shook his head. "I want Noah in my life, and maybe one day I'll have him, but he's doing his life's work right now and I can't stand in the way. It's hard not seeing him, but I believe in us. We'll find a way someday. Or, at least, I'll talk to him about it. But when I do, I'm going to tell him that I'm staying here. Didn't I just admit that things are going well? The only good opportunities for me are the ones right here. How do I apply for that dual citizenship?"

His grandfather wrinkled his brow. "You mean it? Truly? 'Caravelli and Sons?'"

"Technically just the one 'son,' Granddad."

Silvio dismissed that with a wave of one hand. "Bah," he said, "'Sons' sounds better." Christian rolled his eyes and almost laughed.

Silvio smiled, real joy shining forth from his eyes, but not without a hint of sadness. "It would be my pleasure. I cannot deny how nice it would be for an old man to pass on his legacy. 'Caravelli and Sons.' I never thought, in my lifetime."

"Excuse me," said one of the workers, stepping in through the pool door off the kitchen. "I am... interrupt?"

"Not at all," Silvio said in Italian, slowly enough for Christian to follow. "What is the problem?"

"No problem, sir," the worker replied, also speaking slowly. "I was using the guest bathroom and I found something. I think maybe the young man who was here a few weeks ago may have forgotten it. Should I give it to you? Post it somewhere?"

"I'll take it," Christian replied. "Grazie."

The worker brought him a small wooden box, and Christian recognized it at once. It was indeed Noah's, one of the little boxes that he knew his love had used to store index cards full of wine descriptions. He'd been afraid it might be something important or urgent, but it wasn't. He knew Noah had properly documented all his index cards in his spreadsheet, so leaving a box behind wasn't a problem.

He couldn't deny that it was nice to hold a little something of Noah's, though, especially not knowing when they'd see each other again. Something that, unless Christian misjudged its value, Noah was unlikely to want shipped all the way back to the States.

"What is it?" his grandfather asked.

"One of Noah's little boxes," he said, catching the emotion in his voice too late to do anything about it.

"Ah yes, for the index cards, the wine, yes? May I see?"

Christian nodded, handing the box over to the older man. Silvio popped open the little brass latch and opened the lid. At first he looked puzzled, then he smiled.

"What?" Christian asked.

"Oh, my boy," he replied, his voice quiet, almost reverent. "Your Noah was saving something far more precious than wine."

He handed the box to Christian, who took it and looked inside. In the box was every single note he had written to Noah, first the breakfast ones and then the lunch. A physical, tangible, undeniable record of their love affair.

He shut the box and stood up. "I have to see how the pool is going," he mumbled, and his grandfather waved him off. He did check on the pool, more of a walkthrough as he passed the pool area to get to his room, where he shut the door a little harder than he meant to. He set the box down on the dresser and stared.

The truth was inescapable: he was temporarily homeless. One of his parents would probably take him in if he asked, but Christian didn't want to ask. For one thing he was mad at both of them, and for another he had come to like the feeling of being his own man, of accomplishment, that he had found in Tuscany. Try as he might he couldn't imagine what would happen to that feeling if he went back to the US. Really, once the job at the villa was over he only had two options. Either blow a bunch of his pay on an apartment in hopes that working with his grandfather would pan out, or go back to living with the old man in his cramped little house down in the village. So much for being his own man.

The thought grazed his mind that if he asked, Noah would probably take him in. That thought led him back to the small wooden box, and the tears that had been building finally burst free.

CHAPTER 20

NOAH'S FIRST impression of the old brownstone was "money." Somehow, though, given the last few months, that wasn't as impressive as it had once been. Two months living in the lap of Italian luxury and then another two weeks at home but not having to work left him unintimidated.

Entering the house museum and finding a cocktail party going on, however, did ruffle him more than he liked to admit. He scanned an eye over the men in expensive suits and the women in small chic dresses, desperate to ignore the flannel shirt and cargo pants he'd chosen to wear. He'd chosen them specifically because they were the kind of paint-speckled work clothes one might expect of an artist. He'd even borrowed the shirt from Brendan.

Suddenly a tall, balding man with small spectacles who looked old enough to be his grandfather walked by, and Noah recognized his contact immediately.

"Excuse me, are you Dr. Barletta?"

The man stopped, eyeing him curiously for only a second before recognition dawned across his face.

"Ah, indeed, and you must be Noah!" He reached out a hand and the two men shook. "I've heard so much about you from the Cunninghams!"

That relationship still keeps paying off, Noah thought, but he knew better than to say it. Instead he spent a minute gushing about how good they'd been to him, how helpful and kind, and how lovely their Italian home was. All the kinds of obsequious things he figured a museum curator would want to hear a lowly art student saying about a wealthy family that loved art.

"Ah yes, delightful people," Dr. Barletta agreed. "And I even hear they had a hand in you getting that Melton grant. The name of which you not-so-casually dropped into our phone conversation?"

"I hope you didn't get the wrong impression."

Barletta laughed. "Not at all, not at all. I was, ah, delighted to hear from you. The Cunninghams are real patrons of the arts, in the old sense you realize, of course, and any protege they've taken under their wing is someone worth knowing to a man in my position."

Noah blushed. "I'm glad to— I mean, well, yes. They've been very kind." He looked around at the ongoing party. "I hope I haven't come at a bad time."

"Not at all." Barletta waved a dismissive hand. "We're hosting a small fundraiser for… something or other, I'm afraid I don't know which one. I'm just the curator. They hardly tell me anything. Since whatever it is has apparently been important enough to drag the New York art scene to our little museum during their lunches, however, you should know that you might get a few looks. There are Melton people in the room, you know."

Noah tried to calm his heartbeat.

"Ah, at any rate," Barletta went on, "you've come to see some of the lesser known Florentine artists, yes? Well, not *lesser* artists, of course."

"Of course not." Noah shook his head, eager to get the conversation back to something he was confident about. "I hope I didn't give the impression that I don't respect the work. But you know how it is, Dr. Barletta. Everyone who goes to Florence or who even thinks about Florence, all they want to talk about is—"

"Michelangelo," Barletta finished his sentence, nodding as he did so. The nod turned to a shake of the head. "It's a true shame. Don't misunderstand me, of course, ah, Buonarotti did some of the greatest work of the period. His reputation as one of the greats of Italian renaissance art is very well deserved. But behind that shining sun sit many beautiful others in eclipse, if you know what I mean."

167

It was a very poetic way of describing it, but Noah did, so he nodded.

"Did you have a particular interest?"

Noah cleared his throat. "I've been to the Uffizi, and to the National Museum of Bargello. So I have had a chance to study up."

"Ah, so you've seen the famous Botticellis and Donatellos? Indeed, when you said you were interested in lesser known Florentine artists, I had hoped you wouldn't consider those luminaries for such a list."

"Certainly not. But I heard it through... well, through the Melton grapevine, that your museum happens to have a few of Gentile da Fabriano's pieces."

Dr. Barletta's eyebrows both went up, and Noah relaxed for the first time. He'd impressed the fellow scholar.

"Ah, well, why, we do have a few pieces, as it happens," he said, then he chuckled. "That 'Melton grapevine' is a powerful thing indeed, isn't it? And look at you, the young historian, already learning how to use it to dig out things that are supposed to be a surprise."

"I'm sorry," Noah backtracked, fearing a misstep. "If no one's supposed to know, then we can forget about it. I certainly won't tell anyone."

Barletta smiled again. "No, no, of course you won't. The truth is that we're doing a small exhibition of his work at the end of next month, and we have pieces from around the world right now. It should draw in quite a crowd and, well, a museum like ours...."

"Could always use the ticket sales," Noah agreed. "Your secret's safe with me. In fact, if I find any way to publicize it when it happens, I'll do it."

"Fair enough!" Barletta said, offering his hand once again for Noah to shake, which he did. "Let me show you to the basement."

They took a short elevator ride down into the private lower levels of the museum. Barletta had been right about art being a small world, and his obvious lack of proper dress made him stand out, so Noah did get a few looks and heard his name whispered a few times.

Self-conscious as ever, he was glad when they finally stepped into the elevator to descend.

In the silence as they did so, Noah allowed himself to enjoy the thrill. The ability to just walk into an art museum, introduce himself to the curator, in the middle of a fundraiser no less, and be granted access to areas which were off-limits to the public... because they were a secret! It was everything his nerdy little heart had ever desired.

At the end of the elevator ride, Barletta guided him down a short, dusty hallway to where the few da Fabriano paintings were being guarded and prepared for display. He showed Noah the *Madonna and Child* that the artist had painted around 1400 C.E. and was on loan to the museum from Berlin. They saw the *Coronation of the Virgin*, also on loan, but from the Getty Museum in Los Angeles this time. There were others, each behind climate-controlled glass, but they stopped when they came to the *Miracle of the Pilgrims at St. Nicholas' Tomb* so that Noah could lean in and take a closer look.

"This is one of the *Quaratesi Polyptych*, specifically one of the *predella*, isn't it?" he asked.

"Ah," Barletta said. He pushed his glasses up on his nose to scrutinize as well. "It is. You have an excellent eye and knowledge of the finer minutiae of Florentine art!"

"Not exactly," Noah said without looking up. "I've seen the other nine. This is the one I haven't seen."

"You've been to the Pinacoteca Vaticana?"

The note of surprise in his host's voice didn't fly over Noah's head, but he cheekily decided to lean into it. He nodded again, adding, "And the Uffizi Gallery, as I mentioned. And the one at the National Gallery in London. This is the last one left, isn't it."

"It is," Barletta said. "On loan to us via a friend of mine at the National Gallery of Art in Washington, DC."

The two spent a minute studying the piece together.

"The *Quaratesi Polyptych* are at the center of the work I want to do," Noah said, unable to hold himself back. "The pieces were used as inspiration for some of the first commercial drawings of the region."

"Commercial?" Barletta asked, his nose wrinkling as if Noah had forced him to say a dirty word. "Why in the world would you want to study commercial art?"

Noah chuckled. "You might not understand."

"Young man." Barletta launched into a pedantic voice that Noah knew well from his professors, then also launched into an equally familiar lecture about opportunity and how rare it was to get a chance to really study the artists of the Italian renaissance. Especially for one his age, especially with someone else footing the bill... the "especialies" went on and on. When he stopped for a significant breath, Noah stood up and wheeled around.

"Thank you, Dr. Barletta," he said, offering his hand once more to shake. Barletta took it more out of surprise than anything else. "The opportunity to see this collection has been marvelous. I greatly appreciate it. I promise you, when I make my proposal to the Melton committee later this week, I'll be sure to drop your name as someone who helped me. And, uh, I'll find a way to mention your exhibition when it happens. But not before."

"Not before," Barletta echoed. He'd clearly caught on to the fact that the meeting was over, but Noah couldn't tell if his smile meant he was glad he'd be getting free publicity or just glad to be rid of an inconvenient grad student. Either way, he guided Noah back to the elevator, and Noah was soon back out on the streets of the city.

CHAPTER 21

"AND YOU'RE sure he wasn't hitting on you?"

"Christian!"

Christian laughed to himself. After finding the box he had a good cry, but then threw himself back into his work. He had spent the whole day waiting to call Noah, another long day of tiling a pool and fixing up the villa, and here he was jeopardizing his whole relationship by teasing his boyfriend.

"You wouldn't joke if you saw him," Noah said over the video link. "He was old enough to be my grandfather, tall and skinny. He was—"

"Gay?"

"Yeah, probably, but who cares? Because he was not hitting on me!"

"Okay... I don't have to get territorial, do I?"

"What, you're going to come to New York and pee on me so the other gays will know I'm your bush and not theirs?"

There was an awkward pause. Just long enough for it to go through both men's minds that no, Christian wouldn't be coming to see him any time soon.

"What about—"

"What if we—"

They both laughed.

"You first this time," Christian said.

"The Melton grant has a good stipend attached to it," Noah said. "And funds for travel. What if I find a reason to be in Florence?"

Christian perked up. "Could you— I mean, do you think that's possible?"

"Sure." Noah shrugged. "Why not?"

"I don't know. I mean…."

"What?" Noah sounded nervous.

"I wouldn't want you to go out of your way, is all," Christian said.

"Babe," Noah replied, leaning forward in bed until his face took up the whole of Christian's screen. "You're not out of my way."

"Not like that. Like, I don't want you turning down other opportunities just to come to Florence. Or what if they found out you were coming here just because of me?"

"Well it wouldn't be just because of you." Noah sat back and settled in for comfort. "I mean, I want to see you, but it would be for work. I'd be in and out of Florence art galleries and churches, like, all of the time."

"All the time?"

"A lot of it, yeah."

There was another awkward pause.

"How about this," Christian said. "I'm helping Granddad build the business up, but there's going to be some money when the check clears for the Cunninghams. Not enough for me to visit you in New York, but maybe enough for me to spend a week with you in Florence? Whenever you're in Florence?"

Noah's eyes brightened. "That'd be fantastic! I don't know yet when I would be there, if I can even get there, but I'm working on it. We'll figure it out."

Truthfully, to Christian's ears, it sounded disappointing. He'd been in long-distance relationships before, and they often degenerated into variations on "I don't know" and "We'll figure it out." Variations that never came to pass. Christian knew with all his heart that he loved Noah, that they had a special and unbreakable bond. But there were times that bond felt stretched further than even an unbreakable one should go.

As agonizing as it had been, though, his mind was made up. Noah had his Melton grant but Christian had Caravelli and Sons. Misleading though the name might be he felt confident that it was his surest ticket to a successful future. He hated thinking of it that way because it felt so selfish, as if he was putting his own well-being

172

above their relationship. But he had been watching as his parents' arguments over alimony and shared property heated back up again, and the biggest lesson he had learned was that if two people couldn't be happy as individuals, they couldn't be happy as a couple.

And then Noah smiled at him, from thousands of miles away, and his doubts drifted away like smoke on the wind. He reminded himself that even weeks later Noah was still here, was still answering his calls. They were both still finding a way.

"I miss you," he said.

"I know. Believe me, I know."

Their conversation turned to the villa again, Christian excitedly explaining that the pool was almost done and that Noah would have to see it in all its glory. He was still frustrated, though, and he sensed that Noah could tell. Unlike Noah, there was nothing he could do that might bring them together again. There was no "trip to New York" in Christian's future, it just wasn't financially or realistically possible. Even spending more than a few days in Florence was out of the question. He hated the fact that all the weight of bringing them back together was on Noah's shoulders. Those shoulders were already supporting the weight of having all his dreams come true, and Christian didn't want to be the one to sour those dreams.

Well, he hoped as their talk stretched into the night, *maybe not all of Noah's dreams came with some art grant.*

CHAPTER 22

"COME ON," Brendan wheedled. "Come ooooonnn!"

Noah sighed. He looked up from his laptop, pushed his glasses up his nose, and sat back against the headboard of his bed. He'd been hard at work on his proposal for the Melton grant committee, and he almost had it where he wanted it. He only needed a few more ducks in a row in order to wow not only them, but possibly Christian too. It had been his sole focus for the last few days, but now his temporary British roommate was standing in the bedroom door, dressed for a night out, pleading with him.

"I keep trying to get you to go out, and you keep shooting me down," he said.

"Other people might take that as a subtle hint," Noah replied.

Brendan sighed, not a light little exhalation like Noah but an exasperated, melodramatic emptying of the lungs that caused him to drag his body halfway down the doorframe along with it. Noah rolled his eyes.

"You've been working hard ever since you quit your job," Brendan said, "and that's right admirable. You've already got the grant. They love you. They're not going to take it back or something."

"No, but I need to prove to them that I know how to use it." *And maybe find my way back to Christian at the same time.*

"Of course, and you should be proud. I know how hard it is to get money in the art world, I've been rejected for the Melton twice myself. But all work and no play, y'know? You need to be a well-rounded person for that kind of crowd, which means you need to get out of this place. It's doin' your head in."

174

"My head's just fine. Haven't had any complaints."

"You know what I mean."

"Yeah, Brendan, I know exactly what you mean. And hey, let me guess, this party you're going to, is… I don't know… Blake going to be there?"

Brendan's flinch was all the answer Noah needed. He folded his laptop completely and tossed it aside on the bed.

"Brendan, I like you well enough and all, but I need this to stop. Seriously. I'm in a relationship. Respect that."

Looking a little mollified, Brendan sat on the edge of the bed. The next time he spoke, his voice was more restrained. "I'm sorry to be the one to say it but… are you, though? You talk to each other, but you have no idea when you'll be together again. And sound carries from your bedroom way better than you think it does, mate, so I know that half your conversations are full of apologies for one keeping the other awake."

Noah sniffed but said nothing.

"I'm sorry for trying to set you up," Brendan said. "Maybe it's my own bad luck with long distance in the past, but I'm not sorry for trying to get you out of this apartment once in a while! You have this amazing opportunity that I don't think you fully understand: you are an art student who doesn't have to paint anything or wait tables! Or phone home to your bloody parents every five days asking for cash!"

Noah laughed despite himself, having heard a few of Brendan's video chat conversations too. Brendan laughed with him.

"Come with me. I'm serious. Have a good time. You deserve it. When I see Blake, I'll tell him to give you space."

"Well…." Noah considered. As obviously self-serving as his argument was, Brendan did have a point about staying well-rounded. "I can't stay late. I have to be up early tomorrow. You know that."

"Yeah, yeah, the bloody Melton committee needs to hear how smart you are and give you a check, I know," Brendan said. He grabbed Noah by both hands and pulled him up out of bed. "Get dressed."

Noah did, his one concession to Brendan's advice that he "not dress like he's going to a fucking funeral" being a tight pair of jeans that showed off what Christian liked to refer to as "his assets." Brendan led him to a friend's place, which turned out to be a converted loft, full of people talking and mingling with some kind of metal-jazz fusion playing in the background.

No sooner had they arrived than Brendan abandoned him, of course, leaving Noah on his own to navigate his way to the bar. Once there he asked the volunteer bartender what they were serving and winced when he was told there was "a white," "a red," and "the punch."

As he was considering what could possibly be in "the punch" and whether it was likely to knock him flat and render him unable to present to the committee the next morning, a different but equally familiar British voice spoke up over his shoulder.

"He'll have a glass of the white," Blake said, neatly falling onto one elbow and leaning on the bar, smiling at Noah as if he'd already had a couple himself. "But he'll want to know what it is."

Noah laughed politely and agreed. "I'm a wine snob," he told the bartender, unashamed. "I'll drink whatever, but show me the label."

Smiling back, the bartender nodded, presenting Noah with an empty bottle for display. Noah's eyes rolled so far back in his head they felt like they'd come loose.

"Not good enough?" Blake asked.

If someone paid more than six dollars for this then they got robbed, Noah thought, but it was a maxim of modern wine lovers that "cheap" didn't necessarily mean "bad," so he shook his head.

"It'll do," he said, and accepted his glass. He thanked the bartender with a smile, a silent acknowledgment that the quality of the vintage wasn't the poor volunteer's fault, then took a sip.

"Did I guess right?" Blake asked.

Noah briefly considered discussing his preference for red and the reasoning behind it, but decided there was a chance Blake might consider it an invitation, so he just nodded.

"Sure, I'm easy," he said.

"Not what I heard." Blake winked.

Noah realized that in his haste to avoid offering an invitation he had, in fact, done just that. He coughed on his wine, stepping away from the bar as he did so, and Blake followed.

"Sorry," Blake said, "if I'm being forward. But you know how it is these days, especially in this city. You don't ask, you don't get."

"Sometimes you don't get even if you do ask," Noah said under his breath.

"What was that?"

Noah stopped by a window, enjoying a cool breeze that was cutting through the late summer New York air. He turned to Blake, wineglass still in hand, and figured if he was ever going to ditch this guy, he would have to be direct.

"Look, Blake, you seem like a nice guy," he began. "And I don't know what Brendan told you but... I'm in a relationship right now."

"Well... good to know," Blake replied, sounding entirely unsurprised, taking a sip of his own white wine.

"Brendan did tell you, didn't he."

Blake took a deep breath. "He said you met someone while you were in Italy, yeah, and he said that you were trying to have a go of it. I'm sure you two talk every day, send each other little romantic international packages, have a meetup scheduled for the next time you can both afford to get away, right?"

"What's your point?"

"I respect it, really I do," Blake said, leaning in a little closer. "But... he is over four thousand miles away. And I'm right here."

Up close Noah could see the trace of stubble so closely shaved on Blake's chin... his breath smelled like oak barrel aged white wine, nutmeg, and mint chocolate. His smile was rakish and seductive.

"Just tell me you'll think about it?" he asked. "I've done distance, love. It doesn't suit people like us."

"You just met me," Noah protested weakly. "There are no 'people like us' that you know of."

"Oh, I think there are," Blake said. Then Blake kissed him.

Noah's shock was immediate and overwhelming, but he'd be lying to himself if he said it wasn't a good kiss. Blake's tongue explored his mouth, and that little devil on Noah's shoulder reveled in the chance to taste that mint chocolate rather than just smell it. For one shameful moment that he would carry for years, he enjoyed it.

When the kiss broke, tears in his eyes, Noah took a step back. Blake smiled. So Noah slapped him.

Never having hit anyone before, or at least not since fighting back against a schoolyard bully in grade school, Noah surprised himself. The noise it made was like a sharp pop from a firecracker and he realized he'd hit Blake so hard that his own hand was red and throbbing a little.

Blake just stood there looking at him, stunned, a handprint reddening on his face. Noah watched as his surprise turned to fury, and only then did he notice that all eyes at the party were on them. So he did the only thing he could think of before Blake had a chance to take a swing back at him. He flung the glass of wine in Blake's face.

The thought flashed through his mind that Blake looked ridiculous, fuming, his face turning red, dripping with cheap white wine, and he finally understood what it was that all those women on television found so satisfying.

"Keep your hands to yourself!" he shouted, then stormed for the door. Brendan reached out a hand to stop him, but Noah flung it away. He was on the verge of tears all the way back to his apartment, and once there, he threw himself into bed and let them come.

In the morning Brendan was nowhere to be found, but Noah's alarm clock went off just the same, so he forced himself up. The memory of the previous night's encounter still stinging in his mind, he dressed professionally, grabbed his things, and headed out the door. Twenty minutes later he was at the university, seated on a bench in a stuffy academic building hallway.

It's all riding on this.

Noah was more nervous than he could ever remember being, but he did his best to hold it all in. Most of the files for his upcoming presentation were on his computer—he had been promised a wireless connection he could use to give PowerPoint on—but he went over the few pieces of actual paper in his hands to make sure he wasn't missing any. He found that two were in the wrong order, and putting them right actually calmed him down more than upset him.

The university hallway was deserted. Presumably students were in class or whatever, Noah couldn't even think. The only thing he could concentrate on was the door across from where he was sitting, a wood door with frosted glass inset that read "Melton Grant Office."

He realized he was anxiously tapping one foot and stopped.

"Get it together," he told himself under his breath.

Things with Christian were starting to gnaw at him. Their love had indeed been strong enough for distance, it seemed, since over the last few weeks not a day had gone by without a call between them. But when would they see each other again? The longing for comfort, not just emotional but physical, was agonizing. At first Noah told himself it was just a sex thing, that he'd gotten accustomed to having a little nookie whenever he wanted it. Unwilling to even consider the idea that their relationship was purely physical, they'd engaged in a few "spicy" calls together, and it had been nice enough. But his right hand didn't hold him afterward and whisper sweet nothings in his ear.

I have to have Christian back. He steeled himself. *And this is the way to do it.*

"Excuse me, are you Noah? The grant recipient?"

Noah shook himself out of his reverie. A young man about his age, presumably another graduate assistant, had stepped out of the committee room and was addressing him.

"Yeah, I mean, yes, that's me."

The young man smiled. "They're ready for you."

Noah took a deep breath, picked up his things, and went inside.

The assistant guided him through an office area, down a corridor past some private offices, and into a wood paneled conference room. They were in the heart of the building, with no natural light, a perfect spot for him to make use of the projector screen that had been set up against the far wall. The lack of natural light made it just the sort of room Noah preferred for presentations, but it also made him think of Christian. All those beautiful windows back at the villa. Against his will he had a few inappropriate thoughts about his naked lover lying back, snoozing on the bed, the light of the morning sun cast over him.

He physically shook himself to snap out of it. Standing in front of a panel of art experts wasn't the time to be picturing Christian's beautiful, luscious.... *Stop it!*

This isn't a time to picture him, he thought to himself. *It's time to get him back.*

There were about a dozen people seated all around an oval conference table, and he wasn't surprised to recognize the face of Mr. Chester Cunningham. Among the sea of otherwise impassive faces his was a calming port, giving Noah a light smile and even a small thumbs-up as he walked past them toward the screen.

"Good morning, ladies and gentlemen," he began. "I'd like to take this opportunity to thank all of you for your faith in me with this grant, and for taking time to hear my proposal this morning."

The man at the head of the table, far across from where Noah was putting down his laptop and shuffling his papers, spoke up. "Mr. Andrews, let me say on behalf of the grant committee that we were very impressed with the initial proposals you outlined in your application. If what you have for us today is as intriguing as they were, then this will likely be a very short meeting indeed."

A few chuckles passed through the room, and Noah felt the tension in his shoulders relax. It was going to be okay.

It took a few minutes working with the assistant to set up his laptop and get it connected to the projector, but soon his first slide was on the screen. When he went to hand out the papers he'd brought with him, executive summaries of his proposal so that each member of the committee could follow along like an agenda, the assistant eagerly took them from him and began to distribute them. Noah saw heads nodding, but he couldn't tell if they were impressed at his thoroughness or if they had been expecting something like this and would've been disappointed if he hadn't offered it.

Either way bringing it was a good thing, he thought. *So here goes.*

"I'd like to begin with the *Quaratesi Polyptych*," he announced, showing the first slide. It depicted the *Madonna with Child and Angels* for which da Fabriano was well known. "I'm sure everyone here is familiar with da Fabriano's work, but just in case, the *Polyptych* was made for the Quaratesi family chapel at the church of San Niccolò Oltrarno in Florence, Tuscany. This piece, the central piece of the display, also bears a medallion with the image of the redeemer above it. This one is in the National Gallery in London, but I was lucky enough, with your help, to see one of its companion pieces at a local museum just recently."

Noah took a deep breath. He'd demonstrated that he knew what he was talking about, not just the artistic merits of da Fabriano's work but the historical relevance also, and what's more that he knew how to use the money and connections of the grant to further his work. He hoped it would show competence (and confidence), and from the looks around the room, he wasn't disappointed by the reaction.

Now came the hard part: convincing them that the work's commercial value had relevance and was worth studying in and of itself.

"What not many know, and what my presentation will show, is that da Fabriano's work for the Quaratesi family held not just religious significance, but commercial significance as well. The Quaratesi family, like many other wealthy families, obviously wanted a work by a prominent artist hanging in their family's chapel at the local church. But as my research will show, they wound up using it for a very different purpose also."

He moved to the next slide and was both gratified and relaxed by the sound that came from the audience. From the darkness, Cunningham smiled at him. Several of those present emitted slight gasps, as if they had just been shown the true significance of something they'd seen a hundred times before.

Which, Noah supposed, they had.

"Another way in which the Quaratesi family was like other noble families," Noah said, "was their vineyards. Many significant vineyards, actually, vineyards that produced bottles just like this one. I have to thank one of your members, actually, someone present here even now, for the opportunity that allowed me to take this photograph. Let me advance to my next slide and we'll look a little closer...."

Ten minutes later he could feel them eating out of the palm of his hand. Twenty minutes after that and he knew they were sold. He could practically see the visions dancing in their heads of the book he would write and they would publish as a definitive study. At the end of the hour when the lights came up, they were standing in line to shake his hand, chatting among each other as they did so.

"Amazing," Mr. Cunningham said when he took his turn. "I never would've thought of it. If there's anything I can do to help, just let me know."

"Actually, there is something," Noah said. "Something you can do that no one else can do."

"Name it!"

I'm coming, Christian, Noah thought. *I'm coming.*

CHAPTER 23

A WEEK after his grandfather's visit, Christian was finally ready. The villa was done.

The final inspection had gone perfectly. Each room, each piece of architectural art, all had been lovingly restored, and the house was declared "up to code and a work of art to boot," the exact words of the inspector. He had insisted on shaking Christian's hand, much to the pride of Silvio Caravelli, whose puffed-up chest showed that he would not have missed such a moment for the world.

For his part, Christian too felt the pride of a job well done. All his sadness was gone as he contemplated this new direction in his life. The Cunninghams would appreciate all his hard work, he was confident that the workers would all speak well of his leadership, and he'd found a new passion for work with his hands that he'd never expected to find in his old life of partying and lying around.

Well, he considered, *maybe not all the sadness.*

He pushed thoughts of Noah out of his mind as he walked back up the gravel drive toward the house, focusing instead on where this new direction might take him. When the inspection was done and the inspector was gone, he and his grandfather had spoken of the future.

"My boy, this could mean big things for us, very big things," his grandfather had said. He'd broken open a bottle of white Chianti that he claimed to have been saving for a special occasion, and sitting on his granddad's beat-up old sofa, Christian accepted a toast. The wine was almost cloyingly sweet, but he got it down.

"What's the next step, then?" he asked.

"Well, I'm already working on the new website," Christian replied. He had shown his grandfather what it looked like on his phone, using the old man's spotty wireless connection, and Silvio seemed impressed. "Social media isn't up and running yet, but I'll do that next."

"Caravelli and Sons, back in business!" his grandfather cried, rising in his chair from excitement only to crash back into it again with a grimace on his face. He thumped his leg with one hand. "If only this were healing faster, I would be out there with you."

"Granddad, you're doing just fine. You hardly even need the cane anymore."

"Bah." He held up both hands as if envisioning a marquee. "A lifetime of experience guiding young, strong hands into the future!"

"We're gonna have to work on that slogan, Granddad. It's not going to hashtag well."

"Don't talk back." He raised his cane menacingly, and it was all Christian could do to keep from laughing. "We must also get you your dual citizenship. I know some people in the government, your father knows some people in America, we make it happen."

Christian nodded, taking another sip of the sweet white wine so as not to look impolite.

"You know," Silvio mused, "once you have that, you can come and go as you like. Maybe vacation in New York now and then."

"And who has money for that, Granddad?"

"We will! As soon as the business is up and running again."

It had seemed like a fantastic, foolproof plan as his grandfather outlined it there in his living room, but as he walked back up the driveway to the Cunninghams' villa, Christian's doubts haunted him again. For one thing, how many old houses in need of renovation like this one were they going to find? Especially ones with American owners who had a fat open checkbook?

It's a beautiful dream, Granddad, he thought. *But it's gonna have to start off a lot smaller than that.*

He envisioned home repairs, contractor work, lots of heavy lifting in the summer, mud in the spring and the fall, and living off savings and odd jobs in the winter. As different as it seemed from the life he'd led in Miami, as many creature comforts as he saw himself having to do without, it still appealed to him. He smiled to himself. It would be hard work, but it would be his own.

Christian arrived at the house to find the doors still unlocked, for which he chided himself. The alarm system had been installed, he should've locked the doors and set it when he left that morning. Bad habits were hard to change, apparently.

He ran through the list of final tasks in his head. He had to pack up his personal stuff and clear out, check if the pool guys had left a tarp over the pool and put one down if they hadn't, schedule the cleaning ladies so they could work the place over before the Cunninghams arrived, do one final walkthrough, and leave the keys on the little table in the foyer. He would retain one front door key and a code to the alarm, in case he needed to get in during an emergency before the Cunninghams arrived and also to let the cleaners in when they came. But soon the Cunninghams would come take ownership, he'd hand the key over, and that would be that.

He anticipated needing about an hour, most of that spent cleaning his personal effects out of the big guest bedroom. He shut the door behind him and got to work.

No sooner had he pulled out his duffel bag, though, than his cell phone went off. It was his grandfather, and a flash of panic went through his mind. He'd seen the man not half an hour ago, but the older Caravelli had been drinking and was still not good on both legs. He rushed to answer the phone.

"Christian!" Silvio cried out of the little speaker, "Christian!"

"I'm here, Granddad. Is everything okay?"

"Stop whatever you are doing, my boy, right now!" he shouted. "Drop everything and call Signore Cunningham. He just called me, and he must speak with you urgently!"

Urgent? He's over four thousand miles away. What the hell could be so urgent?

"Okay," Christian said. "I'll make sure I call him. Let me just—"

"No!" his grandfather shouted vehemently. "You call him right now! I will hang up and call back in thirty seconds, and when I do I had better hear a busy signal or you'll feel my cane!"

Click went the phone, and the line was dead.

Christian rolled his eyes. *What could Chester Cunningham possibly want that upset Granddad like that,* he wondered. *Maybe he changed his mind on the new color scheme I wanted to paint the exterior....*

It was a thought, a nice one because it would mean at least a few more days' work on the villa before he had to leave it, but not one that would explain his grandfather's agitated state. Resigning himself that he'd better call right away, Christian dialed country and local codes and then the number. The comical image of his grandfather, chasing after him up and down the Italian hills in an effort to cane his backside made him laugh only a little. He believed the old man would at least make an effort to do it.

On the other end, all the way in New York, Cunningham answered on the second ring. The line was nice and clear for a change, but Christian walked over to his bedroom's french doors to try for the best possible reception.

"Hello? Is this Chris Caravelli?" Cunningham asked.

"Christian, yes, sir," Christian replied. He tried to be polite and a little deferential when talking to his employer, but being called anything less than his real name had begun to bug him lately. He blamed Noah.

"Ah, yes, of course," came the officious voice from the other end. "I hope everything's going well out there."

"Absolutely, sir, you caught me as I was starting the final walkthrough. The cleaning service will be in once more before you arrive, I'll supervise that, and I'm packing my bag as we speak to get out of your beautiful guest bedroom. Thank you again for letting me stay here while the work was in progress."

"Of course, of course," Cunningham said. "Nothing to it. We saw the pictures, and you did marvelous work. I don't know if your grandfather told you, but I told him that there'd be a bonus included when the final payment goes from our account to yours."

Christian raised both eyebrows. While he didn't consider the Cunninghams stingy, not after installing all that custom tile for them, he hardly considered them generous either.

"Well, thank you very much, sir, and no, Granddad didn't tell me anything. Except to call you, that is. He made it sound like you had something you wanted to talk about."

"Oh," Cunningham replied, and for the first time since Christian had known him, the man sounded as if he didn't know what to say next. "Oh, well, I had assumed he'd have filled you in. Either him or our... uh... representative."

"Representative?"

Cunningham chuckled on the other end of the line. "Yes, I thought that at least might have piqued your interest. So you really don't know why I asked you to call?"

Christian was becoming a little frustrated and tried to keep it out of his voice. "I'm sorry, sir, but I really don't. Is there something more you need done with the villa?"

"In a manner of speaking," Cunningham said. "You said you were beginning your final walkthrough, is that right?"

"Yes, sir."

"How about this: call me when you've finished, okay?"

Christian was thoroughly confused, but he nodded. "O-okay. Is there something I should be looking for?"

Cunningham laughed again. "Oh, you young people. You'll know it when you see it."

Click went the phone, and the line was dead.

Freakin' everybody's hanging up on me today, he thought.

Christian poked his head in the other guest bedrooms, and all were immaculate, just as he'd left them. He went into the study, the library, the master bedroom, everywhere. From the master bedroom he peeked out the double-glass-paned doors to the patio and garden, even they were spotless. Unless a bomb had gone off in the kitchen, he didn't know what to expect.

When he walked into the kitchen, sure enough, he found the unexpected. Wrinkling his brow with surprise, he took stock of the three suitcases, one of them quite large, piled up near the little dining table.

Then he heard the splashing from the pool.

As soon as Christian stepped through the kitchen door and out into the courtyard, a body was visible doing broad underwater strokes away from him toward the far end of the pool. The swimmer was completely immersed but visible through the crystal-clear waters in the light of the afternoon sun. He was lightly tanned except for his bathing suit area, an obvious fact given that he was completely nude.

Before he could stop himself, Christian actually put a hand over his mouth in surprise and delight. He realized that he would know that ass anywhere.

When he reached the far end of the pool, Noah put both hands up over the lip and hauled himself out. Christian watched his lover pulling slowly up and onto the concrete, drops of water running in rivulets down his hair, his back, the dimples above the adorable globes of his behind. Startled at himself, Christian found that while the moment was undeniably erotic, he was hardly overcome with lust. The joy at seeing Noah again flooded his whole being, filling him with warmth that could be nothing else but love.

Unashamedly still naked, a far cry from the shy young man who'd first arrived at the villa months ago, Noah continued to drip as he walked over to the glass table and poolside chairs next to the decorative fountain. It had Noah's glasses on it, and a bottle of wine with two wine tumblers. He put on his glasses and turned around to face Christian. The tip of his penis was still dripping with water, and Christian felt what he believed Noah must've felt that first time he'd walked in on Christian in the shower. A desire to both have and to hold, in every sense of the words.

Noah smiled. Christian broke the silence.

"What—what are you doing here?"

Noah shrugged. "Couldn't think of anywhere else I'd rather be."

Christian began walking around the pool toward him. "But… your grant. New York?"

Noah shrugged again. "They loved my proposal. I'll be spending my grant doing the first definitive study on the art of Italian wine labels."

Christian's jaw dropped. "You're… you're kidding. That sounds ridiculous."

"Actually, the Melton folks are pretty excited about it. Chester talked me up a bit, and I asked if I could start out here at his amazing wine cellar before moving on to some private collections in Florence, a couple of museums that normally don't even let students in, and then… wherever."

Christian reached Noah, who despite the afternoon warmth was shivering just a little due to being naked and wet and outside. Christian folded his arms around the other man, freely offering whatever warmth he had to give, and Noah gratefully accepted.

"That's… that's amazing. I'm so happy for you. We'll still get to see each other, at least."

Noah pulled away and looked up at him, his eyebrows confused but his mouth already smiling. "When I heard you on the phone with him, I assumed Chester had given it away, but he really did leave it for me to tell you, didn't he?"

"Leave what?"

"The Cunninghams aren't going to be able to come to the villa," Noah told him. "Not till next year. They asked me to ask you to stay on as a caretaker. Room and board still provided, and a monthly amount. They… they might have thought I needed looking after."

Visions of a year with Noah in Tuscany, sharing the villa and sharing his bed, danced through Christian's head with ecstatic intensity. Somewhere off in the distance, he was already starting to picture how he might get on one knee under a starry night next summer and ask Noah the question he knew he was even then ready to ask.

It made Christian's head spin, in fact. It was a lot to take in. "Why won't they be coming? Is there something wrong with the house? Did… did I do something they didn't like?"

Noah shook his head. "Apparently Mrs. Cunningham broke her leg. I heard she fell off a horse."

Christian leaned back and laughed long and loud, resounding off the walls of the courtyard. Noah insisted the irony wasn't funny, but it wasn't long before he joined in. When they were done he kissed Noah, the full and passionate kiss he had told himself he would give if ever he got the chance again, and Noah responded in kind. They held the kiss as long as they could, each wanting to break apart and contemplate a long future together but neither willing to separate at all.

When they finally did come up for air, Christian looked down into Noah's beautiful blue eyes. "What now?" he asked.

Noah pursed his lips and raised one eyebrow. He let go of Christian with one arm and used it to gesture to the bottle of wine and the glass tumblers on the nearby table.

"A glass of red?"

SAM CARLSON was born in the suburbs of Chicago in 1981 and caught the writing bug early. From writing plays and poems in grade school through to earning degrees in theater and English from Northern Illinois University, he's written across several media in his career in order to refine his talents at crafting the best and most interesting characters.

No stranger to long vacations with a certain special someone, Sam has always enjoyed seeing other countries, touring vineyards and wineries to sample the local vintages, and seeing art in the finest museums that will allow an uncultured Midwesterner like himself in through the doors. A lot of those include restored home museums, which was the real genesis of this book.

A Glass of Red is his first title published with Dreamspinner Press and his first published novel. Despite being a newcomer to the romance genre, readers of Sam's work are always eager to describe it with words like "touching" and "hilarious." Sam hopes he can provide a funny (and steamy) experience that will take your breath away.

All the wines and wine pairings mentioned in this book were the result of meticulous personal research, and are highly recommended (to responsible adults, of course).

Sam can be found on twitter @SCarlsonAuthor, where he tries to stay out of arguments with authors that are wiser than him. He can also be found in his native Chicagoland, where he still lives with his husband and their two cats.

CPSIA information can be obtained
at www.ICGtesting.com
Printed in the USA
LVHW021731110521
687113LV00013B/1112